Praise for Sleepless Summer

'Dehouck creates a melancholic and wistful atmosphere in a world dominated by dark egocentrism. Uncanny, original and haunting'
Flanders Literature

'Following the lives of various inhabitants of a sleepy village who, increasingly rapidly, turn their surroundings into a living hell, is one of Stephen King's trademarks. Dehouck is better at it—without involving the occult or taking up more pages than necessary'
NRC Handelsblad

'Dehouck obviously loves the written word and manipulates it with impressive precision. It is a small miracle how he brings to life over twenty characters in barely two hundred pages'
Het Parool

'A gem. With *Sleepless Summer*, this Flemish writer proves that his award-winning book *De minzame moordenaar* ('The Mild-Mannered Murderer') wasn't just a one-off success'
Algemeen Dagblad

'A worthy successor to *Reservoir Dogs*'
Knack

'*Sleepless Summer* is a surprising book that exudes an atmosphere of melancholy. The minute descriptions of the events in the village lead almost unnoticed to a furious finale'
Thrillerweb

'Masterly. Definitely worthy of the Golden Noose prize'
Vrij Nederland

'A tragicomic novel about a small community that is increasingly disrupted'
MPO Books

'It's like the blackest version of *Midsomer Murders* you could possibly imagine, infused with the dark, psychological tinge of the finest Scandinavian crime fiction. I loved it'
Raven Crime Reads

'A compact and original story, with a heart-stopping denouement. Dehouck writes sparingly and concisely. With the right words in the right place, he only needs a few pen strokes to get to the heart of his story. A beautiful book, a relief'
JURY, GOLDEN NOOSE AWARDS

'In this book everything is exactly right and everything is the result of something else. *Sleepless Summer* is really well written and equally well conceived'
De Lees Fabriek

'The language is compact and effective; this is a book that never bores. A beautiful, compact, universal, and exciting story about how a seemingly insignificant occurrence can lead to unprecedented disaster. Bram Dehouck once again proves his talent with this exciting and often comical novel'
Misdaadromans.nl

'An incredible story in which everything is perfect'
Thrillers Leestafel

BRAM DEHOUCK (Belgium) was the first author ever to win both the Golden Noose and the Shadow Award, the two most prestigious prizes for Dutch crime writing, for the same novel: *De minzame moordenaar* ('The Mild-Mannered Murderer'). *Sleepless Summer*, his second novel, was again awarded the Golden Noose and the Knack Hercule Poirot Public Prize, and was nominated for the Crimezone Best Thriller Award.

JONATHAN REEDER, a native of New York and longtime resident of Amsterdam, enjoys a dual career as a literary translator and performing musician. Alongside his work as a professional bassoonist he translates opera libretti and essays on classical music, as well as contemporary Dutch fiction by authors including Peter Buwalda, Adri van der Heijden, and the forthcoming *Two Blankets, Three Sheets* by Rodaan Al Galidi. His recent translations include *Rivers* by Martin Michael Driessen (winner of the 2016 ECI Literature Prize) and *The Lonely Funeral* by Maarten Inghels and F. Starik.

Sleepless Summer

BRAM DEHOUCK

Sleepless Summer

Translated from the Dutch
by Jonathan Reeder

WORLD EDITIONS
New York, London, Amsterdam

Published in the USA in 2019 by World Editions LLC, New York
Published in the UK in 2015 by World Editions Ltd., London

World Editions
New York/London/Amsterdam

Copyright © Bram Dehouck, 2011
English translation copyright © Jonathan Reeder, 2015
Cover image © Mischa Keijser
Author's portrait © Charlie de Keersmaecker

Printed by Sheridan, Chelsea, MI, USA

Library of Congress Cataloging in Publication Data is available

ISBN 978-1-64286-016-0

First published as *Een zomer zonder slaap* in the Netherlands in 2011 by De Geus

Twitter: @WorldEdBooks
Facebook: WorldEditionsInternationalPublishing
www.worldeditions.org

With thanks to Femke Beerten, Sarah Lingier
and Dorothee Cappelle

Drinking in the morning sun
Blinking in the morning sun
Shaking off the heavy one
Heavy like a loaded gun

What made me behave that way?
('ONE DAY LIKE THIS'—ELBOW)

THE DRAMA IN Blaashoek began as all great dramas do: with a trifle.

Immediately following the tragic events, sociologists and psychologists scrambled to pinpoint the cause of this human cataclysm. Loneliness, cried one. Alienation, bellowed the next. Small-town insularity, opined the third. It was only a matter of time before a fourth would come up with inbreeding.

It was much simpler.

The town's demise was brought on by a well-meant project supported by statistics, spreadsheets, measurements and calculations. No one saw it coming. No one could have known.

The root of it all was an eighty-four-word item in the local newspaper:

> FIRST WIND FARM IN BLAASHOEK
> The province and municipality have licensed alternative energy provider Windelectrix to erect ten wind turbines along the Blaashoek Canal, on the outskirts of the town of Blaashoek. Windelectrix hopes to complete the construction of Belgium's first wind farm before the

summer. 'Our surveys have indicated this as the most suitable location,' according to chief engineer Didier Deroo. 'It is not only the optimal site for generating wind energy, but the chance of causing a nuisance or disturbance is minimal.'

Perhaps the word 'minimal' should have alarmed a few people. But it did not. According to some survivors, the trail could be traced back to the butcher Herman Bracke. In fact, everyone's troubles started more or less at the same time, but for the sake of convenience let us begin with the butcher.

1

Monday

Herman Bracke lay staring at the window. The orange light that shone through the pinholes in the metal roller shutters danced to the rhythm of his breathing. Herman looked from the window to the black of the ceiling, not pure black but a collage of dark specks. He closed his eyes in an attempt to get the specks to amalgamate into the black hole into which he hoped to sink, but his exhausted brain conjured up another image, the bane of the insomniac. Herman Bracke saw a sheep.

Mutton is underrated meat, Herman thought. He himself preferred it to the far-too-young beefsteaks that were so popular lately. Where were the days when beef was allowed to age properly and did not have to be baby-pink in order to sell?

He was now wide awake.

Herman sighed. He turned over. The orange specks left a vague blue impression behind his eyelids. They no longer danced. They hummed. Like flies around a turd.

They had been humming for five nights now.

It all seemed so optimistic last week, when the ten Windelectrix turbines officially went operational. There had been a mass migration from the big city and the surrounding villages for the inaugural festivities. The turbines towered over Blaashoek like enormous idols. Speeches by the mayor and the minister fluttered away in the wind that from that day onward would provide Blaashoek with power. The mayor's ego did not stand a chance against the whipping blades. They hogged all the attention, impressive as the rotors of invisible airships.

Only Herman's sausage stand equaled the success of the turbines. Craning their necks made people hungry, and soon enough the crowd thronged his kiosk. Not only the sausages did well that late June evening: Herman's famous pâté sandwiches were gobbled up too. Bracke's Blaashoek Pâté, that was the name of his pride and joy, although the locals called it 'summer pâté'. What they called the delicacy did not concern him much; all that interested him were the compliments it received—such a refreshing pâté, how *do* you do it?—and his wife Claire particularly enjoyed the rewards the specialty of the house brought: the trip to Spain, the swanky Audi and the landscape pond they had had installed last year in the garden. They could afford a city break just from that evening's profits alone.

The turbines were a blessing for Blaashoek, Herman thought, as the mayor, himself the beefy type, bellowed with laughter above the crowd. Herman imagined the thousands of tourists the hypnotizing blades would draw. Thousands of tourists who would work up an appetite from peering upward. Thousands of tourists who would relish Bracke's Blaashoek Pâté.

But even then Herman was disquieted by a menace he couldn't quite put his finger on. 'You look like you're afraid the thing'll come crashing down on your head,' the mayor had laughed, his face swollen from years of consuming beer, cheap champagne and savory snacks, while Herman handed him a napkin to wipe mustard off his chin.

Herman simply nodded and turned his gaze back up toward the imperturbably rotating turbine. Its dizzying height hurt his neck, and the reflection of the evening sun on the blades made his eyes itch. He had to admit he was overcome with the absurd fear that the colossus might indeed snap off. He saw the blades sag forward and then come thundering down with a metallic shriek he recalled from the film *Titanic*. There was no time to scream as they spun downward like maple-tree whirlybirds and obliterated dozens of lives in one fell swoop. Blood and pus spattered from the mayor's cleaved body like the mustard from the bun he still held in his hand.

'How 'bout it?' The rudely worded order shook Herman from his daydream, and he dutifully speared a sausage. 'Cool, huh?' the young man said, nodding upward, as he walked off. Herman nodded back. The blades were still firmly attached to their shaft. What an idiot he was.

When he lay in bed that night, satisfied at having sold every last sausage and slice of pâté, he thought at first there was something wrong with the refrigeration unit.

'Do you hear that?' he asked Claire, who had rolled herself up in the bed sheet.

'*Don'earathing*', she mumbled.

He pulled on his trousers and tottered down the stairs to the butcher shop. There was nothing wrong with the refrigeration unit. But when he returned to the bedroom, the noise was still there. It sounded like an idling car. Herman knew he should just ignore it, otherwise he would never get the rumble out of his head. So he rolled over, closed his eyes and thought of Bracke's Blaashoek Pâté. A superb name for a superb product. How do you make it so refreshing, the thousands of tourists would ask. It wouldn't be long before ...

Now the humming sounded like an idling truck.

Ignore it.

Perhaps he should convert the garage into a small delicatessen, with a rustic interior to give the impression that it had been around since Grandfather Bracke's day, where the tourists would savor the pâté and other specialties. He could ask the tourist office to distribute his flyers. Blaashoek had put itself on the map, and if he played his cards right his butcher shop could stand to benefit. He would discuss it with Claire in the morning, but for the time being ...

The hum seemed to crescendo.

That first night, tossing and turning, swearing under his breath, Herman realized that it was not an idling car that kept him awake. Nor was it a truck. It was the wind park.

Claire said he was exaggerating. She had chortled contemptuously when he mentioned it the day after the inauguration. 'You're imagining things, Herman, those turbines don't do anything except go around in circles. The heat must be getting to you.' Case closed.

The humming continued the second night too, and the third, and the fourth. Every one of those nights he tossed and turned until the sheets chafed his skin, he threw off the covers like a dead weight, shuffled out of the bedroom and went down to the living room to watch TV. One news bulletin after the other passed through his exhausted brain. At daybreak, after a cloying announcer's weather report, he dragged himself to the butcher shop. Every day the fatigue assaulted his disposition anew. Every evening he vowed to ignore the turbines. On the third night he used earplugs, but he heard the turbines through them, amplified by his heartbeat. The earplugs plopped gently against the wall when he flung them angrily into the darkness. Claire raised her head, snarled what in God's name was he up to, turned over and fell back asleep.

Now, five nights after the festivities, he once again lay staring at the ceiling, and caught himself stupidly musing on the virtues of mutton.

Claire snored with drawn-out snuffles. She slept right through the hum. Perhaps thanks to the numbing effect of the white wine. Until six days ago, Herman snored too. His hand glided over the bulge of his belly and hooked itself under the elastic of his pajama bottoms.

We're too fat, he thought. We're both too fat, and that's why we snore.

A useless thought in the middle of the fifth useless night.

◆

Postman Walter De Gryse liked the tingling pain in his legs. The wind from the Blaashoek Canal caught him from the side and yanked on his handlebars. It did not bother him in the least. He could have used a motorbike or a car, if only to save time. But he had been given permission to deliver his route by bicycle, rain or shine, until his retirement. Or until his body gave out.

For Walter, the daily bike ride from the main post office to Blaashoek and back was the best remedy against minor infirmities. His body consisted of bone, tendon and muscle. There wasn't an ounce of fat on him. In his twenty-five-year career he hadn't taken a single day of sick leave. Not a single day! This did not make him popular with his fellow postmen, who had all unanimously cheered the introduction of motorbikes and delivery trucks. While Walter happily mounted his bicycle for the seven-kilometer trip to Blaashoek, they grumbled and groused about the new routes and lit up a cigarette as soon as the foreman was out of sight.

The wind made Walter's eyes water and sucked snot out of his nose. He cleared his throat and spat a wad of phlegm onto the grassy shoulder. He righted himself, looked across the water and saw the turbines. Beautiful, the stately way they dominated the landscape. The same wind that rattled through his spokes was being converted into electricity. Marvelous. Fifteen years ago, as chairman of the action group 'No Nuclear Waste in Blaashoek', Walter took up arms against the government, which was planning to dump radioactive garbage in this haven of natural beauty. At home he kept a scrapbook with all the newspaper clippings from back then. The construction of the wind park in his town felt like a personal victory over nuclear energy and the dark forces intent on propping it up. He shifted to a higher gear to allow the pedals to turn at the same tempo as the turbine blades.

The turbines were beautiful for another reason as well. They reminded Walter of the coast, where as a child he always spent the last week of the summer vacation. For hours on end Walter would build sand castles and dig moats, which to his delight filled with water at high tide. Then he had a *real* fortress, surrounded by a *real* moat that no one else could cross. And it was only truly finished when he had carefully placed the paper windmills on top of his edifice. How often had his cursing father dragged him from the beach, because back in their stifling efficiency apartment dinner was getting cold while Walter sat gazing at his little windmills at sunset. After a school year full of tedious bookwork, he yearned for the sea, the sun and the paper windmills.

Later, when he outgrew windmills and his interests shifted to bikinis, he dreamt of exotic oceanic tableaux with waves that made the North Sea look like a puddle. But he never got to see palm trees and pearly-white beaches. His youthful romance with Magda—and particularly her unexpected pregnancy at age seventeen—kept him in Blaashoek. For twenty-eight years now they had lived in her home town, which compared to the Shangri-las of his dreams was no more than a sandbox where toddlers jealously eyed one another's sand-cake stands.

In the sandbox of Blaashoek, Walter was the kid with the smallest bucket. Practically everyone in the town lived with the comforting thought that there was always someone less well-off than they: Walter the postman and his little woman Magda. It did not bother him, he was content. He and his puny bucket had also built dream castles.

Shortly after Laura was born he went to work as a postman. Barely a year later Lisa completed the family. The girls' upbringing took a big chunk out of the family budget, but conscientious bookkeeping meant he and Magda could afford to give them a happy childhood. Walter took great pleasure in planting little windmills atop his daughters' sand castles during vacations at the beach. At *Sinterklaas* they always got less than they had hoped for, but were content to play with the cheap toys. Lisa wore Laura's hand-me-downs without grumbling. Thanks to all their economizing they were able to send both daughters to university. Now Laura earned twice what he did, and if Lisa got her promotion next year she would earn three times as much. His daughters' busy schedules prevented them from visiting regularly. He regretted that. Money alone did not buy happiness.

Walter glanced over his shoulder and pulled onto the two-way road just before the Blaashoek exit. He took the first curve and banged with a short *kadunk* onto the sidewalk. Time to deliver the mail.

◆

Herman heard the familiar *klunk* with which, every workday, Walter coasted up onto the sidewalk. He had to grab hold of the delivery van. He looked at the half-pigs that dangled from the meat hooks like abstract artworks. His eyes wouldn't focus. The meat seemed to swell and the van shrink, or vice versa, and the dead meat's delicate odor, much reduced by the refrigeration, turned his stomach. He was tired, dead tired.

'Just bills for you today,' he heard Walter say. Herman let go of the van and took the envelopes. The electric company's logo floated on one of them. The address consisted of vague, dark flecks.

'Thanks,' he said.

Walter looked into the delivery van and sniffed.

'Mighty cozy in there.'

Herman smiled and looked as well. Now he saw the cadavers in razor-sharp relief. Then they went all blurry again.

'Magda'll come by later to pick up some of your pâté,' Walter continued. 'Set aside a nice big slab for her.'

Bracke's Blaashoek Pâté. Herman realized he urgently needed to whip up another batch. Today.

'I'll be going, you've got your hands full here,' Walter said, placing his foot on the pedal, ready to push off.

'Do you hear them too, at night?' asked Herman.

Walter took his foot off the pedal.

'Pardon?'

Herman hesitated.

'Do you hear them too, the turbines?'

In Walter's face were the eyes of the gaping sheep.

'Do I hear ... I'm not sure I get your drift.'

'I thought maybe you also ... that you ...'

Now Walter looked as if he felt the cold metal of the electric pistol in his neck that would turn him into a lamb chop.

'Never mind.'

The postman squeezed Herman's shoulder. 'You take these little piggies to market, and I'll deliver a few more bills.'

He winked and rode off. Herman followed the sinewy body and the dark mop of hair, and wondered if he was the only one who heard the turbines. That couldn't be. Surely the drone deprived someone else of a good night's sleep? The awful idea that he alone lay awake night after night, that he alone endured that torture, made his spine stiffen. As though he dangled in the delivery van among those hunks of meat.

He looked over the rooftops and saw them.

'Monsters,' he muttered.

◆

A new girl had come to live in the subsidized housing. Walter inspected the name on the envelope. He peered through the letter slot, as though she might be standing there on the other side, waiting for him. Nothing but an empty hallway. He smiled at his own foolish thought, pushed the letter through the slot and rode, whistling, to the next mailbox.

◆

Saskia Maes did not wake up from the clatter of the letter slot. She had already been awake for about an hour, waiting for the moment that she might hear the postman, in the almost unbearable hope that he would not pass her by again today. She had given up waiting for the clatter; the hope had turned to certainty that today, too, she would receive no answer. Why would anyone go to the trouble of writing her a letter? Letters got written to important people. Not to a nobody like Saskia Maes. No, she had to face facts: she stood at the bottom of the social ladder. Not on the second rung, not even on the lowest one. She was a piece of lint under the mat where people wiped their feet. That is what she was thinking when Walter De Gryse pushed an envelope addressed to her through the slot.

She sprang out of bed, threw on her bathrobe, ran—skipped—through her ground-floor apartment, opened the door and peered into the hallway. There it lay, just behind the front door, a white rectangle that beckoned her the way a banknote beckons a homeless person. She trotted into the hall, the blood flowing thicker and faster through the veins in her throat, and her eyes latched onto the envelope. She was halfway through the hall when she got a massive slap in the face. Not from an open palm, but from the realization that the letter was not for her. She stood still for a moment. The letter was for Bienvenue, the Senegalese asylum seeker who lived upstairs. Of course! How could she be so stupid as to think otherwise? Because you just *are* stupid, a voice in her head answered.

She gingerly approached the letter, her legs wobbly and her eyes fixed on the still-illegible address. Then she noticed that the name above the address was short. Too short to be Bienvenue's unpronounceable full name. Her heart leapt. And then she saw it clearly: 'Ms. Saskia Maes', in elegant feminine handwriting. Underneath: 'Blaashoekstraat 27'. There should have been an 'A' after the number, because she lived in apartment A and Bienvenue in apartment B, but that was a technicality. Now more than ever it was just a detail, now there was proof that someone considered her worth writing to, and that within a few seconds she would know what they had to say. Above the address was something else that made her heart skip a beat: the logo of the insurance company in the city. It was the letter she had been expecting for days now.

The envelope tore open under her nervous fingers.

The letter was folded neatly into thirds, with only the address, the date and the salutation visible.

Dear Ms. Maes, it said. They called her 'Ms.', and 'Dear'! A wave of pride flowed through her body. That pride evaporated when she read the rest of the letter.

Dear Ms. Maes,

Thank you for your interest in the position of secretarial staff member. We have studied your application thoroughly and I regret to tell you that your qualifications do not meet those necessary for this vacancy.

We will keep your résumé in our files for future reference. Should there be an opening more suited to your profile, you will be most welcome to submit a new application.

Yours sincerely,

Severine Baes
Director, Personnel and HR

Severine Baes, what an impressive name, Saskia thought, although she had no idea what HR meant. She folded the letter back into the envelope and shuffled to the apartment. Severine Baes's last name might differ from hers by just one letter, but their lives were worlds apart. She could understand it, the rejection letter. They had studied her résumé and had come to the only logical conclusion: that she was not fit to participate in society. Her initial pride sank in her stomach like a hunk of congealed fat. She was stupid, homely and useless. And a weakling, for she was unable to hold back the tears. There was only one thing she could do: crawl back into bed and allow Zeppos, her three-month-old cocker spaniel, to lick her tears dry.

◆

There was no pâté. Magda De Gryse already saw as much. She was third in line at Herman's Quality Meats, after old Mrs. Deknudt and the wife of that stinking-rich veterinarian Lietaer. Her relief at the refreshing coolness of the butcher shop was short-lived. While Mrs. Deknudt read out her order she had plenty of time to inspect Herman's deli counter. After allowing her gaze to drift over the farmer's brochettes and country steaks, she noticed a gap between the Beauvoorde pâté and the chopped liver. That gap was where the summer pâté—or what Herman rather ludicrously called 'Bracke's Blaashoek Pâté'—should have been. But now there was a gap as empty as the skull of her dear Walter.

She sighed and had a good look at Herman, who by mistake had just wrapped up 500 grams of steak tartare instead of ground beef, and had to start again. When he reached over the counter for the container of tartare, his hair fell in greasy strands over his sweaty forehead. His hands trembled. His usually rosy cheeks were pale, while the swollen skin under his eyes was a gruesome shade of purple. He settled up with Mrs. Deknudt. Where was Claire, anyway? Off shopping for dresses in the city again?

'Really, Herman,' Deknudt said, 'now you've given me back a twenty instead of a ten.'

'Oh, sorry,' he mumbled.

There was something the matter with him. He seemed ... drunk.

'Herman, there's no pâté,' Magda said as Mrs. Deknudt folded the ten-euro bill into her wallet and before Dr. Lietaer's wife could order. She gave Magda a dirty look, but Magda ignored her. Madame Princess could just wait.

'I haven't had time, Magda. I'll make a batch later today, if I get the chance.' He wiped the sweat from his forehead with his sleeve. He rubbed his eyes, as though he were about to cry.

'I hope so, Herman.'

He sighed.

'They make quite a racket, don't they, the windmills,' he said. The three women looked at him sheepishly, Mrs. Deknudt because she was stone-deaf, that bimbo Lietaer because every spring she fried her brains on a tanning bed, and Magda because she had misunderstood Herman's comment.

'Your meat mill, you mean?' she asked, biting her bottom lip to keep from asking in jest if he'd been tilting at windmills. He did not answer. He grunted and like a zombie took the Lietaer woman's order. Of course only the most expensive cuts of meat were good enough—no country steak for her, it *had* to be sirloin.

Magda was so nonplussed by Herman's wretched appearance that she ordered country steaks instead of the breaded Swiss patties Walter liked so much. On the way home she fantasized about what had worn Herman out so. It couldn't be Claire's lust. She smiled. Liquor, that must be it.

Her irritation about the lack of summer pâté made way for a blissful warmth. For the first time in ages, she had something to be cheerful about.

◆

Zeppos was the ideal antidepressant. When Saskia came sniffling back inside, Zeppos darted under her bathrobe to lick her feet. Giggling, she led him to the sofa, where he slobbered all over her calves and behind her knees. Tears of sorrow became tears of laughter. She even got a little aroused by it.

Now that she was in the shower, she could look on the bright side. Tomorrow she had an appointment with the social worker, and although she was nervous about her reaction to the job rejection, there was good news too: she was in somebody's files! For the first time in her life, people thought she was worth keeping on file. Maybe the insurance company would offer her another job. A secretarial post was perhaps aiming too high, but she would be happy to deliver the mail or answer the phone. Moreover, she was quite the speed typist. Of course, she still made oodles of mistakes, and she could always brush up on her grammar. At any rate, being kept on file was a first step.

She turned off the faucet and got out of the shower, more refreshed than before, as though the water massaged not only her body, but her thoughts too. What's to complain about? She had been given this beautiful apartment, even though instinctively she felt she did not deserve it.

She hastily finished her bathroom routine. All her life Saskia had been stuck in a whirling carousel of guilt, retribution and labor, worked ragged like a beast of burden during the day and scorned as a downright nuisance during her meager free time. Pleasure and relaxation were for namby-pambies. But she had escaped from that nest of vipers and tried, once in a while, to enjoy life.

'Come, Zeppos,' she said, 'time for our walk.'

She did not need to call him, he sprinted toward her of his own accord. She stroked his brown head while he licked her hand. He's a lick addict, she giggled to herself.

'Have you eaten up all your food, Zep?'

She peered into the kitchen. Zeppos's dish was as clean as a whistle.

'Let's go then.'

Before pulling the door shut behind them, she glanced around the apartment, at the living-room suite she had bought with the last of her savings, to make it feel a bit like *her* apartment, at the cabinet where the compilation CDs were neatly arranged next to the old CD player, at the round dining table with the cheap chairs. She cleaned house at least twice a week. The sober interior meant more to her than just a collection of thrift-store furniture. Here, she decided things for herself. Here, no one could harm her.

◆

Zeppos sniffed around lamp posts and doorsteps, wagging his tail, and occasionally lifted his leg to offer the Blaashoekstraat a sign of his appreciation. Saskia's feelings swung between the enjoyment of a summer stroll and the acrid guilt of not really deserving this little pleasure.

Then she heard a car approach. She froze and flattened herself against a wall.

'Zep, come,' she hissed, and the little dog cowered at her feet. She dared not look, and turned her face to the wall. She heard the rattle of the old engine, recognized its sound. She braced herself for squealing brakes, the slam of a door and her furious grandfather's screams and blows. Her escape from the ugly past was about to come to an end, with Granddad dragging her into the dirty green Mercedes, back to the farm. Back to the life she deserved.

The car slowed, then picked up speed and drove past. It *was* in fact a Mercedes, but a clean blue one. Saskia felt her heart sink back into her chest. Her breathing returned to normal. But the fear would never pass. She was constantly on edge, took the putt-putt of a lawnmower for Granddad's jalopy, or her heart skipped a beat every time a Mercedes drove by, like just now.

She had to put it out of her mind. She watched Zeppos's carefree sniffing and tried to enjoy the warmth of the sun on her face. She'd been living in the town for three weeks now—if you could call a street with a hundred houses at most a town—and she was getting to like it here more and more. The first time she rode into Blaashoek on the bus, something struck her as strange. Along the Blaashoek

Canal were ten tall poles, like chimneys from an underground factory. But no smoke came out, and the sight had something surreal about it. The poles appeared to have no use whatsoever. All they did was spoil the view of the countryside.

A few days later she realized that they were not chimneys at all. Silly me, she thought, when she saw the blades rotating in the air. She had to admit they couldn't have found a better place for the turbines: a persistent, potent wind blew over Blaashoek. Even now she felt it tug at her clothes, like a child nagging for candy.

Despite its modest size, Blaashoek offered its inhabitants all the amenities you could want: there was a butcher shop—the butcher was a jovial fellow, and his wife always politely nodded hello—and a small grocery, where the manager Patricia was always up for a chat. Saskia liked the town's casual friendliness.

The neighboring pharmacy was the one place she unconsciously gave a wide berth. She hoped never to have to set foot inside. Since learning what the pills had done to her mother, she couldn't walk past a pharmacy without a chill running down her spine.

The only drawback was the poor bus connection to the city, just one per hour. Tomorrow she'd have to take the 7:15 bus to make her appointment with the social worker. She would love to have a car, but didn't know how to drive. Who would have taught her? Granddad said women behind the wheel was about as good an idea as pigs in a cockpit.

Her daydream had led her further from home than she'd ever been until now. She didn't like going out much, and if she did, she usually chose the other side of the town. She glanced around.

'Oh, Zeppos, look!' she said. The dog skipped expectantly

toward her, but returned to the flower planter when it became clear he was not going to get a treat. Saskia squinted in order to read the brass nameplate across the street. JAN LIETAER, VETERINARY SURGEON. The brilliant sunlight gave the hard-to-read letters a golden halo.

'Now we don't have to go to the city anymore for your shots,' Saskia laughed. She pulled Zeppos away from the planter and crossed the road.

◆

The large sliding glass doors in the study offered a splendid view of the backyard. The lawn gleamed: yesterday he had treated it with Evergreen lawn fertilizer. The grass was bordered with lavender, sunflowers, grapevines and juniper shrubs, plants meant to evoke a Provençal atmosphere. Something that worked perfectly on a dry, hot day like today. *Pieris rapae* butterflies—'small whites' in everyday language—cheered up the yard with their romantic flutter. He gazed with fitting pride at the five small olive trees that marked the back edge of the garden. All that was missing was the chirping of the horny cicadas, the mating song that gave most people that blissful vacation feel.

Jan Lietaer sighed, and his relaxed posture—hands loosely behind his back—tightened into a cramp. Irritated, he kneaded his left wrist with his right hand. Since last week his eyes hadn't had a moment's rest. Every two seconds, dark blotches swept like monstrous slugs across the lime-green grass, only to vanish, quick as a wink, behind the fence. The shadows disrupted the orderly composition of the yard, they sliced the meticulously mowed rectangular lawn into irregular wedges as they rotated with the wind. Even more than the fact that they were there, it irritated him that they were there for good. He looked up and sighed again. How could he boast to his friends about the exceptional character of his garden anymore if they were forever being distracted by these ghostly shadows?

Chinese torture, that's what they were. They incessantly assaulted his life's work. And with each new shadow that passed across the lawn, the cramp in his hands became more resolute.

Nice yard, Jan, but those shadows, enough to drive you bonkers! He could just hear them saying it, he saw them laughing up their sleeves, because even though their yards might not be so gorgeous, at least they weren't defaced by some stupid wind turbine. Worse yet, he could just hear his mother, with that icy, pinched voice of hers: a man with balls would have seen to it that they built their turbines somewhere else.

He wanted to sigh a third time, but his breath was cut short by the gentle tinkle of the bell, followed by the sound of footsteps and agitated clicks on the floor. The door to the waiting room squeaked. A client with a dog. He wrenched his eyes off his tormented backyard and hurried to the office.

Jan's practice was on the rocks. Ever since farmer Pouseele's daughter had gone into veterinary medicine, he had lost his livestock clients one by one. So he turned to specializing in house pets, but how many house pets were there in Blaashoek? Three cats and a pair of hamsters. It didn't bother him. Thanks to the generous inheritance from Grandfather and Papa, his practice was no more than a hobby. And once Mama finally went to join dear old St. Peter—and what relief that would bring him—he would have no financial worries whatsoever.

He nevertheless gave his few remaining clients all the attention they deserved. He switched on the computer. He fumbled around in the drawers and laid a few pencils and ballpoint pens on the desk. He opened the filing cabinet and placed three manila folders on the tabletop. There, that looked good.

He went into the hallway and opened the waiting-room door. Sitting there was a mousy girl he did not recognize. She wore cheap clothes—gym shoes, white socks under a pair of wash-shrunk jeans, and an untucked yellow T-shirt whose collar was already a bit frayed. Her auburn hair had been twisted into a short ponytail. Her brown eyes were intelligent-looking but timid. Despite her plain appearance, she was not unattractive. With a little more attention to her looks she would certainly turn a few men's heads when she took the cocker spaniel that lay between her feet out for his walk.

'Good morning,' he said amiably.

The girl nodded shyly, the dog pricked up his ears and leapt up with a short bark.

'Do come in,' Jan said, leading them to the examination room.

He showed the girl a chair.

'Are you new in town?' he asked after plopping into his leather desk chair.

The girl nodded.

'Just three weeks now. I live in an apartment.'

'Ah.' The only apartments he knew of were from the subsidized housing, so he added: 'Let me guess: number 27?'

She nodded and cast her eyes downward, blushing.

'And you live at number 72. I thought that was a funny coincidence.' She stuttered with embarrassment. He thought she was adorable.

'We've already got the digits of our house numbers in common. And a fondness for animals too, I suppose?' His smile relaxed her.

'I'm so happy I can have Zeppos. I take him out for a walk

every day, and when I'm not home I put him in the court-yard.'

Jan nodded.

'You're doing the right thing. A spaniel's terribly cute, but he needs plenty of exercise. A lot of people forget that. They buy a dog and make him spend his whole life in a doghouse. And then they're surprised when he keeps the neighborhood up all night.'

He rolled his eyes as a sign of rapport. The girl giggled.

'I take him out every day, rain or shine, sleet or snow.'

'Good heavens, don't tell me you drag poor Zeppos through snowstorms?'

In just a second her cheeks and neck went blood-red.

'No, no,' she stuttered, her hands folded in a cramp that seemed even more painful than his own hand-wringing as he fretted over the garden. Startled by her reaction, Jan turned to the computer.

'I'll just open a new file, and you can tell me what's up with your dog.'

He hoped she would get over his misplaced joke by the time he had entered her data. The program had finally finished loading—it took forever, it was high time he got a new computer—when the front door slammed shut and he heard the clatter of high heels. The kitchen door shut a bit too loudly, he thought, a sign that his wife did not expect anyone besides him would hear it.

'There, the program's loaded.' He brought his hands to the keyboard. 'I already have your address,' he winked, 'but perhaps you could also tell me your name.'

He had typed just three letters of her first name when the high heels approached. The door to the practice swung open and Catherine appeared half in the doorway. Still, after fifteen years of marriage, her stylish beauty took his breath away. His stomach knotted up when her long blonde hair glided over a shoulder.

'I've got sirloin for later,' she said. He nodded, and only then did she notice the young woman sitting motionless in the chair. The dog had turned toward her and inquisitively wagged its tail.

'Oh, you've got a visitor. I'll leave you to it, I'm just going out. Don't worry about dinner, I'll be back in time.'

Before she closed the door she said 'good day' to the statue that appeared to be riveted to the chair. She suggestively raised her eyebrows.

◆

Panic gripped his heart. The melody of Magda's voice told Walter she was expecting an answer, but he hadn't been listening. He was engrossed in a newspaper article about a court case that would start in September. 'The trial of the century,' screamed the headlines in boldface. A policeman in Ieper had murdered five people in cold blood. Even a year after the fact, he remained remorseless. The international media had got hold of it, and soon enough heads rolled: the Chief of Police and the Interior Minister. The Ieper court had moved the trial to the Expo Hall on the outskirts of town to accommodate the onslaught of press and public. The newspaper interviewed a female expert in criminal profiling who had been called in by investigators. She was quick to note that the local police had bungled the case, like a bunch of amateurs. And that the murderer had brilliantly misled her too, which still caused her sleepless nights.

Walter folded up the newspaper and leaned forward, his arms crossed on the table. He would have been happy to admit his inattentiveness to his wife, but he feared that the punishment for his crime would, as usual, be disproportionate. First a half-hour lecture, and then being made to do the washing-up on his own. He waited for the tirade, but it did not come. Magda batted the dust from the candlesticks on the window sill and simply repeated what she had just said: 'Something's up with Herman.'

Walter recalled Herman's pallid face and vacant look. Magda glanced over her shoulder and saw his attentive posture as a sign to continue. She appeared to be conducting an orchestra with her feather duster. There were no candles in the candlesticks. Candleless candlesticks, what could possibly be more useless?

'It's hardly surprising, what with all Claire puts him through. I saw her the other day in yet another new dress. She's got enough outfits for three a day. And all those trips, they must cost him a fortune. And have you had a good look at that car of theirs?'

Herman's Audi Q7 was a luxurious behemoth, but Walter was not all that interested in cars. He much preferred the bicycle. Magda drove a second-hand Citroën C3, although she regularly dropped hints that an Alfa Romeo or a Volkswagen would suit her better.

'It *is* pretty showy, that car,' he conceded.

'Showy?' She let the foolish word sink in. 'Now that's an understatement. It's a car for multimillionaires! Just think how much pâté and sausages he'd have to sell! And it's never enough for Claire. Always more and more and more. It's killing him.' Walter nodded. He kept quiet, because Magda was on a roll, and she always saved the best for last. She laid the duster on the table and put her hands on her hips. Although he and Magda were the only ones in the room, she lowered her voice.

'He's drinking. I noticed it this morning at the shop. He could barely stand up. He was trembling and sweating like an ... *alcoholic*.' She spat out the last word.

'It can't be as bad as that,' Walter ventured, but she cut him off.

'Of course it's as bad as that. You should have seen it! Incidentally, there was no summer pâté either. Oh, excu-uuuse me: "Bra-cke's Blaas-hoek Pâ-té" was sold out. He's slipping, Walter.'

'And I even asked him to put aside a piece for you.'

'Ah, yes,' Magda sighed, and in that sigh Walter recognized her long-standing frustration that he never got his act together. He couldn't even manage to reserve a slab of pâté from the local butcher. She took the duster from the table and vanished into the kitchen.

'There's a new girl living at number 27.' He counted the seconds before she reappeared in the doorway. It never took her longer than four.

'What's that?'

'There's a new girl living at number 27. Saskia Maes. I delivered a letter for her this morning.'

She let the words sink in. Then she shrugged her shoulders.

'You mean that pathetic skinny thing? She's been there for three weeks. You're miles behind, as usual.'

He blushed.

'It was a letter from the insurance company in the city.'

She did not miss a beat.

'She'll be in debt with them, no doubt.' And then added: 'Does that Negro still live there?'

'His name is Bienvenue. Last week I delivered a package for him.'

'A package?'

'I don't know what was in it. There was no return address.'

'Shady business.'

'He does odd jobs for the town council. And he always nods politely when he cycles into the city.'

'Well, why doesn't he just stay there.'

'He's not doing anyone any harm, Magda.'

'Maybe not, but he's not doing anyone any good either.'

She marched off to the kitchen and added, from the stove: 'except the locksmith'.

Jan Lietaer stared at the garden. He saw the shadows and was repulsed by the sight of them. Then he walked to the living room and stood in front of his gun cabinet, an entirely out-of-place metal monstrosity. Catherine frequently cursed it, but Jan loved it, and loved its contents even more. He opened the cabinet, took a deep whiff of its scent and stroked the guns. The Winchester 70 Featherweight, the Beretta Silver Pigeon III, and his favorites: the fantastic Browning B525 Hunter Elite and his grandfather's old Sauer. All the way down at the bottom lay the crown jewel. Not a hunting rifle, but the Remington Rand M1911A1, a pistol given to him by his father, who had bought it (so he said) from an American soldier right after Liberation. The soldier had shot it just three times—and not killed anyone. Jan had never used the pistol himself, but he maintained it meticulously. He secretly hoped an intruder would oblige him to fire the remaining five bullets. He took the Sauer, the lightest gun in his collection, out of the cabinet, got a six-pack of beer from the refrigerator and went out to the backyard.

Saskia Maes did not notice, as they passed the pharmacy, that Ivan Camerlynck was watching them. The pharmacist stood at the left-hand window, blocked from view by the rack of suntan lotion he placed there during the summer months. In the winter he restocked it with cough syrup and throat lozenges. Ivan Camerlynck turned up his nose as the girl passed. She strolled as though life were one big vacation. She looked fit and healthy enough to work. But apparently she chose to sponge off the government, to live off taxpayers' money, off people like him who earned an honest wage. She was dressed like a frump. Really, people who had nothing to do all day and didn't even take the trouble to make themselves presentable! But what truly turned his stomach was that stupid animal walking alongside her.

How often hadn't he seen it on TV? Have-nots who moan that they can't make ends meet on their welfare check, but then maintain half a zoo. Okay, the little cocker spaniel was cute, with his floppy ears and waggling backside, but how did that hussy manage to feed it? Ivan Camerlynck ground his teeth. He could well imagine how that floozy financed her extravagances. He hardly needed to spell it out. A blow job for three cans of dog food. Something like that.

That this banana republic of theirs was going to hell in a handbasket was one thing, but he could not stomach the fact that these excesses had now reached Blaashoek. And practically his own doorstep. Ivan Camerlynck sniffed indignantly.

It was all the fault of those good-for-nothings on the city council. What had they got up to the past few years? First they dredged the Blaashoek Canal. What on earth was the point of that? If a cargo ship tried to sail through it, it'd run aground on duck shit within two meters. No, the tens of thousands of euros' worth of dredging projects were invested, according to the city council's report, *to facilitate recreational boating*. Recreational boating, for God's sake! So now the banks were regular mooring spots for small yachts, captained by bloated nouveaux-riches in white trousers and plaid shirts, cronies of the mayor, of course, and undoubtedly just as crooked.

Then when the old lady next door died they bought up the house and turned it into subsidized apartments. He took the occasional peek over the wall. Best to keep an eye on these things: before you knew it they'd be breaking all sorts of building codes. The bathrooms they'd put in were nicer than his. And for whom? Parasites!

His registered letters to the mayor received the usual hackneyed replies. First a woman with two young children came to live on the ground floor. The racket those rowdy little monsters made! Ivan was always on guard when the mother and her quick-fingered rascals came into the pharmacy. One day the woman just vanished into thin air, and a darkie moved into the upstairs apartment. A strapping, well-fed colossus, he hardly looked like an impoverished refugee. And judging from the loud half-conversations Ivan heard through the wall, the man wasn't the least bit concerned about his telephone bill.

And the icing on the cake: a week ago they opened that damned wind park. Ten of those berserkly whirling turbine towers! And what did his fellow townspeople do? Did they protest when they heard of the building plans, all those smarty-pants neighbors of his? Half of them hadn't even read the article by the local journalist, a puppet of the mayor, that had been buried on page three of the newspaper. The simpletons he spoke to about it thought the wind park was a grand idea. It would lift Blaashoek out of obscurity, they said. Blaashoek would become famous for its green energy, they blathered. Finally something actually happened in the town, they yapped. Brainwashed by the hollow words of the powers that be, that's what they were. But Ivan did not consider starting a petition himself, or taking his case to the local media. He kept his head down. It can't always be the same people who raise their voice in defense of the public good. There'd only be a backlash.

With a heavy heart he watched the townspeople flock to the opening ceremony and gorge themselves on the sausages and offal pâté from that pig of a butcher. Imbeciles! If he didn't live here himself, Ivan would say that Blaashoek deserved it.

He sniffed. The girl had slipped into the house. He could barely hear her, that's how deviously she had refined her methods of receiving clients. He left his sentry post behind the rack of suntan lotion.

He went to the lab at the back of the pharmacy, where his antipathy toward the girl made way for a sense of excitement. He was eager to prepare the triamcinolone acetonide ointment for Mrs. Pouseele, the farmer's wife, who suffered from eczema. It was a complex preparation; the ointment was prone to curdling. And Mrs. Deknudt would be coming by for her zinc syrup. Even though that one was a snap, he nevertheless looked forward to it.

He had not become a pharmacist just to sell aspirin, suntan lotion and Band-Aids. For that, you could just as well become a salesclerk. His passion was self-made medicines. Even as a student he had excelled in making suppositories, the trickiest preparation of all. Only with patience, precision and cold-blooded concentration did one achieve the ideal result. It was painstakingly difficult to spread the medicine homogeneously throughout the suppository. Moreover, the pill had to dissolve at body temperature, not at room temperature. First you warmed up the powder mixture until it was completely melted. Then you let it cool off. Proper timing was essential, because the mass mustn't be allowed to solidify. Pouring the preparation into the molds at just the right temperature required nerves of steel. When you finally removed them from the refrigerator, you had to pray that the pills would not stick to the molds.

It had been years since he had made suppositories. When the daughters of the postman Walter De Gryse were young, Magda would bring along a prescription once a week, to his delight. His last suppository customer, he now recalled, was Wesley Bracke, the butcher's son.

◆

Catwoman's sumptuous lips closed around his erection. Her head went gently up and down while her tongue glided along his cock. Her cheeks were dimpled from the sucking action. She began slowly, but her movements speeded up in time with his breathing. She pressed the tip of her tongue against his gland, she sucked along the edge toward the center and flicked her tongue vigorously up and down.

Now it was Machteld, the prettiest girl in school, who was riding him. Her small breasts danced to the rhythm of her hips.

Wes Bracke tugged at his hard penis, which he had swathed in toilet paper. Ever since his mother started questioning the dwindling supply of handkerchiefs from the bathroom cupboard, he had switched to toilet paper. The change had numerous advantages. He no longer needed to hide the stinking, stiffened hankies in his nightstand. The soiled tissue could be flushed, unobserved, down the toilet, and a missing roll of paper was far less obvious than the inexplicable disappearance of the handkerchiefs.

Machteld groaned her way to a climax and Wes spurted his warm semen into the toilet paper. He heaved a sigh, zoned out for a few seconds, squeezed the last drops of sperm out of his cock and cleaned himself up. He put his clothes back on. In this weather Machteld probably wore a tight T-shirt and hot pants, which offered a splendid view of her legs. Wes cursed the summer vacation, because it meant not seeing Machteld for nearly two months. His report card was such that his parents were unlikely to take him into the city all that often, certainly not for a party, and the chance that she would show her face in Blaashoek was zilch.

Wes opened the door and dashed into the bathroom. He dumped the paper into the toilet before dropping his pants to piss sitting down. Experience had taught that after jerking off, he would spray all over the place if he stood.

'Wesley, is that you?'

His mother. He felt his cock and balls tighten.

'Yeah, who'd you expect? And call me Wes, not Wesley.' How many times did he have to tell her?

'Dinner's ready.'

He sighed. He stood up, examined the evidence one last time and then flushed it with a single pull of the handle.

His parents were already sitting at the kitchen table. You would think that, after a day in the butcher shop, sausages and hamburgers were the last thing in the world they would crave, but no, his parents consumed meat by the kilo. Father Bracke tolerated bread, vegetables and potatoes at most as a garnish; a meal was not a meal if it did not include at least one juicy hunk of meat. Tonight, pork chops were on the menu.

Was this the right moment to inform them of his new lifestyle choice? His father did not look particularly good-humored. More like a corpse in a slasher film. But what did it matter? He was going to hit the roof anyway.

When his mother prepared to dish him up a pork chop, he raised his hand in a defensive gesture.

'No chops for me, Ma.'

The slab of meat floated above the table. His mother hesitated, looked over at his father. A drop of grease fell onto the tablecloth.

'Are you sick?'

Wes shook his head.

'I'm a vegetarian.'

The curse his father let out made the glasses in the china cabinet jingle.

2

Tuesday

The sheep bounded up the hillside. Herman panted after it, his eyes fixed on the dark ball of fleece. The liquid concrete that seemed to fill his lungs hampered his breathing, his veins could no longer handle the rush of boiling blood, his head could explode at any moment. He did not know what he would find beyond the hill, but from the sheep's excited trotting he concluded that it must be a paradise.

The sheep turned its head. Herman recognized the face of Walter De Gryse. He reached the top on his hands and knees, tugging himself up on the rough grass that cut into his bleeding hands. His nails broke on the dry earth, and sharp-edged rocks burned through the tender skin on his knees.

At the crest of the hill Herman scrambled to his feet, while the sheep galloped down the other side. He let out a yell. Thousands of wind turbines flapped and whined. An army of lunatics. A swarm of irate bees. At their feet, sheep thronged in a sea of teeming wool. Their bleating had a mocking sound to it.

He screamed.

Everything went black. A black comprised of the darkest possible tints of purple, speckled with shimmering white flecks. His eyes adjusted to the darkness and he recognized Claire in the vague lump next to him. She did not budge. She snored quietly. Perhaps he had only screamed in his dream.

The alarm clock showed 2:13 a.m. This was the first time he had slept this long, about three hours. He knew he could forget about falling back asleep, because as soon as he opened his eyes the humming penetrated his brain like a bad song you can't get out of your head.

Herman swung his legs out of bed and tiptoed out of the room. The shop was closed today, but before he started on the bookkeeping he wanted to whip up a batch of Blaashoek Pâté. The advantage of insomnia was that you never ran out of working hours.

◆

'Come in, Saskia.'

Saskia got up from the orange plastic chair and went into Dorien Chielens's office. The small sign next to the door Saskia had spent the past half-hour staring at said SOCIAL WORKER. The office was spacious but stuffy. The white furniture was meant to establish an air of clinical neutrality. Most of all, the room reflected Dorien's chaotic nature: the desktop was covered with dossiers, and the filing cabinets offered a view of hanging folders stuffed with dog-eared papers. A mild feminine perfume mixed with the delicious scent of freshly printed paper.

Dorien opened a window.

'A hot morning like this means there's a storm brewing,' she said. 'And since there's no air conditioning we just have to put up with the street noise.'

She smiled at Saskia, who sat hunched forward with the rejection letter clamped in her hand. She dared not look at it, because then she would start sweating.

'Where'd I put … your dossier … ah,' Dorien whispered as she pulled a thin manila folder from the bottom of a stack, opened it and gave it a cursory going-through. She had the expression of a doctor who had discovered a horrible disease.

'Did you get here easily?'

'Yes, fine, I caught the seven-thirty bus.'

Dorien looked at her watch and furrowed her forehead.

'I'm sorry we didn't have a place for you in the city. You live in, uh, what is Blaashoek, actually? A kind of subdivision?'

'No idea, sorry.' An awkward giggle escaped from Saskia's throat, but she added quickly: 'I like it there, you know. I'm happy in my apartment.'

Dorien smiled.

'We'll try to find something else for you, but I can't promise anything. It's awfully tight at the moment.'

'It's really not necessary. The people are nice. I enjoy living there.'

Dorien looked at her as though she had just said she liked living in a sewer. Then she slapped her hand on the dossier, like a judge about to pronounce a verdict.

'Well, okay then, all the better. And can you get along with ... who's upstairs again? Freddy ... ?'

'Bienvenue.'

'Ah, that's right, Freddy was before him. M'yeah ... the Senegalese guy. I don't know anything about him, my colleague's handling his dossier. But he's all right, neighborly and all?'

Saskia nodded. 'He's awfully sweet. He helped me put my living-room furniture together. And it's cute how he says *bonjour* when we meet.'

But when he talked, on the phone or when he had friends over, she was scared. Not of him, but of his deep voice. His bellowing laugh made her nearly jump out of her skin. In her experience, a raised voice always preceded a beating, just as thunder followed lighting.

Dorien fanned herself with a sheet of paper.

'And how's your dog? Do you take him for walks?'

'Oh, yes, every day. Zeppos is a darling, he hardly ever barks.'

'Okay, good. Remember to give him plenty of water, we don't want him to dehydrate in this heatwave.'

Dorien smiled and puffed.

'I take really good care of him. I even took him to the vet. He has to have his shots.'

'And could you afford it?' Dorien's question felt swift and hard.

Saskia flushed. An itch on her back began to spread, just like her allergic reaction to Grandma's cheap soap.

'Yes, I had … I put money aside, I still have …'

She stuttered from the nerves. Dorien raised her palms in the air.

'Relax, Saskia. I didn't mean to jump down your throat. I phrased my question a bit roughly. You know we …'

'I've brought my bank statements.' Saskia bent over to reach into her bag, a cloth thing she had sewed herself.

'Stop, stop, Saskia,' Dorien laughed. 'I believe you. No need to prove it.'

Saskia sat back up, somewhat reassured. The rejection letter crinkled in her lap, but she did not notice.

'Speaking of finances,' Dorien continued, 'we've instigated a lawsuit against your grandfather.' She thrust her chin in the air, as though the city council had just decided that he would face the guillotine tomorrow on the town square.

'I'm not sure if that's a good idea,' Saskia stuttered. 'I don't want any trouble … they always took good care of me.'

'Took good care of you? Took good care of you?' Dorien leaned forward. 'They did *not* take care of you!'

Saskia did not understand what she meant. 'I got …'

'Saskia, what your grandfather did, we call slavery. Okay,

they fed you and gave you a bed to sleep in, but that's not enough. A person who works, gets paid, that's how things go in society.'

'Granddad said a woman isn't wor—'

'Nonsense. Nonsense. Nonsense.' Dorien raised her hands. 'What your grandfather told you is pure nonsense. Women are worth just as much as men. You are worth just as much as anyone else.'

Saskia blushed. It did her good to hear that, and deep down she knew it had to be true. She knew it, but didn't feel it.

'We've filed two charges against your grandfather. One, he never paid you for the work you did on the farm, and two, he pocketed your unemployment benefits.'

'Unemployment what?'

'If you're unable to work, the government gives you money. To survive. Your grandfather collected these benefits in your name, but you never saw any of that money yourself.'

That must have been an oversight, Saskia thought. Maybe he had been putting that money aside for her. Granddad was old-fashioned, of course, he had a certain coarseness she recognized in so many of the other farmers who came to the house. But he only beat her when she messed up. If her grandparents hadn't taken her in, she would have withered away in some or other orphanage. The stories Granddad told her about that kind of institution, where for punishment they made you stand in an ice-cold shower all night, or where you were abused by nightwatchmen— even on a day like today, they could fill her with terror. She mustn't complain about her grandparents, who themselves had suffered unspeakable hardship during the war. Grandma's motto had become hers too: work hard and don't complain. 'He who keeps his nose to the grindstone doesn't have time to complain,' she said without looking up from her work, when Saskia once asked why they never went to an amusement park like the other kids at school. Grandma's answer made a deep impression on her. Saskia admired her grandmother's diligence. Whenever Granddad punished her, Grandma was always somewhere else, working. Saskia was relieved Grandma didn't know how many mistakes she made. And if Grandma noticed anything, she would keep the peace by not mentioning it. It felt disloyal to criticize them.

Saskia realized she had stopped listening to Dorien, who with grand gestures was explaining how the system would punish her grandfather for his wrongdoing.

'... we don't know for sure. But we're hoping for the best.'

Then she stopped. In the ensuing silence, Dorien waited for some sign of gratitude. A one-woman ovation. She did not receive it. Saskia felt guilty—feeling guilty was second nature to her—but she did not share Dorien's concept of right and wrong. She felt dirty. She knew that life with her grandparents had become untenable, because she wanted to make something of her own life. But those very yearnings augmented her guilty conscience. The fact that she chose to leave the farm did not mean she was ungrateful, or judged them harshly. She only wanted to forget the past and finally make a go of a future. Without guilt or punishment.

◆

Magda stood waiting at the living-room window. An hour and a half already. First Claire left the butcher shop and drove into the city in the Audi. By tonight Herman's bank account would be another couple of hundred euros lighter. And now that dopey Wesley of theirs stood there dawdling with his bike. Poor kid, his mama was too heartless to give him a lift.

Not that Magda gave a hoot about all that. *He* was the one she wanted to see. Did Herman look as disheveled as yesterday? Maybe worse! Had he finally caved in? She relished stories of arrogant shopkeepers who felt their marble floors sink away under their feet, who had to trade in the Audi for a rusty Hyundai and were forced to sell the villa and move to a dingy apartment block.

Anyone who saw her lurking behind the curtain would say she was crazy, leering at a closed butcher shop all day. But she was convinced that Herman had begun his descent into self-destruction, and would drag his family down with him. And she did not want to miss a moment of that spectacle.

Nothing earth-shaking would ever happen in her own life. She had resigned herself to that. Or tried to, anyway, although she couldn't deny the feeling, on occasion, of having got the short end of the stick. Simple Walter was satisfied with his all-too-simple life, but she knew she could have done better. She'd been blessed with good looks, brains and a charmed life until she went and got pregnant. Perhaps all this would have been tolerable in a different setting, but here she was forced to witness, day after day, how ugly Claire achieved what in fact had been intended for beautiful Magda.

Justice would prevail. Magda felt it. It excited her, got her more wound up than the sultry voices of all those TV doctors put together. If your own life is a failure then nothing beats seeing someone else's life fail even more. She no longer strove for her own happiness, but lived for the unhappiness of others. She had developed a nose for fiasco, for the conceit before the fall. And her nose told her that there was a tasty spectacle in the making. And she had a front-row seat.

◆

Wes was not at all looking forward to the journey. He sighed as he checked the tire pressure. He hadn't ridden his bike for at least a year: there was a school bus, and if he needed a lift into town he could ask his mother, if she wasn't working in the shop.

But the city-bike was his only chance to see Machteld. Even though it felt like the frame was filled with lead, he would ride it to the city every day 'to get into shape'. His parents, those poor morons, probably thought he was cycling thirty kilometers a day, but in reality it was only seven to the city, about three through the most likely streets, and seven back. He would meander around until he bumped into her. In this weather, he was certain, she would strut through the shopping district, flaunting her gorgeous body. What exactly he would say if he did meet up with her, he wasn't sure yet. He had rehearsed a number of scenarios, but maybe it was better just to start with 'hello'. No telling where 'hello' could lead.

And today of all days had to be such a scorcher. He threw his right leg over the crossbar and pushed off on the pedals. His muscles protested. The bike wobbled. After ten or so pumps he finally got some momentum. His tongue already practically hung in the spokes and salty perspiration stung his eyes, but the prospect of the encounter erased all hardship. You had to suffer to snare a woman. At least, if you didn't have good looks or the gift of gab. Wes was even prepared to die for Machteld.

◆

The boy lurched over the bike path. It was unkind to laugh. Saskia watched the awkward cyclist as the bus rode into Blaashoek. The turbines welcomed her with waving arms. It felt good to be back.

When she got off she nodded goodbye to the driver, who

wiped the sweat from his forehead with a large handkerchief.

She had hoped to pick up some farmer's sausage, but the butcher shop was closed. How stupid of her to keep forgetting that. It wouldn't spoil her day. Dorien had said: 'You're worth just as much as anyone else.'

Just as she was about to turn the house key in the lock, the front door to number 27 flew open. A woman tripped over the threshold, catching her balance with a short hobble. 'Hi,' she called to Saskia. She clattered on her high heels over to a car, leaving behind a wake of very feminine perfume. She was pretty: the green dress cut to just above the knee fit snugly on her fine figure.

Saskia watched her car squeal away from the curb. Won't Bienvenue be pleased, Saskia thought as she closed the door behind her, with a visit from such an attractive social worker.

◆

Jan Lietaer shot. The can splattered open in a head of beer foam. He grinned. Normally he first drank the can dry, but it was too hot to start on the alcohol so early in the day. So he took aim at full cans of beer, and it gave him more pleasure than he had expected. Instead of the hollow crack of tearing aluminum, he was now treated to a real-life sound: the can took the bullet like a sated rat and jerked over backward. Beer gushed out like blood from a blown-off head.

He crossed the field to place a new victim on the rusty table. He had bought the field three years ago when its reclusive owner, a farmer's wife, had died. It was adjacent to his own backyard and was the ideal place for rifle practice, in preparation for hunting season.

A veterinarian who hunts? That's like a doctor who strangles little old ladies! How often had he heard jokes like this? He just laughed along with them. Hunting was his passion, and the veterinary practice only a hobby, but he couldn't go around admitting that. Jan had learned to hunt as a boy; his father took him on hunting outings, just as grandfather Lietaer had done for his own son.

Hunting thrilled him. Caring for your weapon, shouldering and aiming it, the excitement of game in the open field, the smell of woods and gunpowder—it was wonderful. He quickly learned that there was nothing he could do about the way man had divided up the animal world, parallel to his own world: into the privileged, the fair game, and those with a death sentence. He may as well enjoy it.

Like a child experimenting with insects, Jan felt both thrill and revulsion. The deed was thrilling, the result revolting. At his first hunt he found a hare whose hind quarters had been blown off languishing under a bush. Its eyes bulged out of its head, terrified and desperate, its frothing mouth gasped for air and its ears were turned toward the barking of the dogs. Ever since, those death throes flashed through Jan's mind every time he took aim. He still hated finding poorly shot game. His fellow hunters put the animal out of its misery, quickly and emotionlessly. It was noble, they said. Yeah, as long as you conveniently forget that you were the cause of that misery, Jan thought to himself.

He eased his conscience by de-worming dogs and splinting cats' paws. The veterinary practice, he reasoned, was a logical extension of his passion for hunting. His atonement. To an extent.

'Are we going to barbecue tonight?'

He turned around. Catherine stood at the garden gate in a pose worthy of a fashion magazine. But she wasn't posing, she was just standing there as she always did, unaware of the beauty she radiated. Each time she leaned against something or appeared in a doorway was a missed photo opportunity. The naturalness, the presence—she must have fallen into a vat of the stuff as a child. He still wondered why she hadn't put more energy into her modeling career, choosing rather to waste her time with his bookkeeping and a bit of volunteer work.

'Barbecue? Mmm, good idea.'

'I'll go into town for some meat.'

'Ah, good. Bring charcoal too.'

'I'm just going to freshen up first.'

She disappeared into the backyard. Jan looked at the beer can. He raised the Sauer, aimed, and lowered the gun without firing. He gathered his things together and went in after her.

◆

They had sealed his ears shut. This radical solution was the only appropriate one, according to the doctor. They used melted sheep fat, because it insulated so well. That was a property he wasn't aware of, but sure enough, it worked. No sound got through. Finally Herman had some peace and quiet! How long had it been? Centuries, it seemed, centuries of humming and burring and droning and thrumming. It was all behind him now, like an exhausting war without winners.

His deafness did not worry him. Claire would no doubt find another way to issue orders. He could install a lamp that signaled a customer had come into the shop. And he could turn on the subtitles for watching TV. No, his deafness was a blessing. He felt liberated, like a village in Normandy clearing up the debris after D-Day.

It wouldn't do to just suddenly appear in the shop with a headful of sheep fat. They would gossip, certainly the first few weeks. But he had to draw the line. Regardless of the consequences. He had never set much store by his appearance. The townspeople too had become accustomed to their odd-looking butcher. Maybe they'd start calling him 'Butcher Sheepfat' behind his back. He didn't care, now that his misery had finally come to a blissful end. Claire could mind the shop more often, while behind the scenes he prepared the famous Blaashoek Pâté.

'Herman!'

He jumped. Did he hear his name? He must be hallucinating. It sounded distant, as though someone were yelling through a metal tube stuffed with rags. A phantom noise, the auditory equivalent of an itch on an amputated arm.

'Herman!'

The sound came from closer now, but it was still muted. His ears would keep trying to deceive him for a while, the doctor had warned, this was to be expected. Those sounds in his head, he simply had to ignore them.

'Herman!' Now the sound of his name was joined by a tug on the shoulder. Was it time to wake up from the anesthesia? Was this the moment they would find out if the operation had been successful? He opened his right eye. He lay, to his astonishment, not on his back in a hospital bed, but on his stomach. No, he sat in a chair, with his head on a pillow.

'What in God's name has happened here? What *is* this?'

It was Claire's voice. The doctor had obviously made a complete mess of it, not only because Herman heard what she said, but mostly because she sounded even angrier than the time the gardener had laid the wrong tiles and had to rip them all out again. When he looked up, his astonishment was complete. He was in the butcher shop. An operation in a butcher shop? That can't be! Claire was justifiably incensed, such a thing was highly irresponsible!

Claire's face hovered dangerously close to his own. He saw her tanning-bed complexion, the mascara on her lashes, the downy blonde hairs on her upper lip. But he paid no notice. His full attention was drawn to her bulging eyes, as though they were glaring at a homeless drug addict who had spent the night in front of the shop window.

Now she brought a dishtowel to his face and wiped a smear of sheep fat from his forehead.

'Leave that!' he shouted. 'It's for my ears!'

'Lunatic!' she shouted back. 'You've lost your mind!'

He felt his forehead and looked at his fingers. What was sticking to it was not sheep fat. It was Bracke's Blaashoek Pâté. Then he looked at the pillow. It was not a pillow. It was a container of raw Blaashoek Pâté. The pâté oozed over the edge, and in the middle was a deep hollow. A hollow with the exact contour of Herman's face. He did not need to check, it was quite obvious.

'Wh-what happened?' he stammered.

'That's what I'd like to know,' Claire ranted, as she swiped at him with the dishtowel.

'I must have ... fallen ... I'm ...'

'You're a *fool*!' Claire whipped him in the face with the dishtowel. When she pulled it back, spatters of pâté flew off him in gentle arcs.

'I guess I dozed off,' Herman muttered. 'I'm ...'

'An idiot, that's what! Just look at this! How long have you been lying here snoring in your own pâté?'

Herman looked around him. His hands trembled. His entire body shivered.

'What time is it?' he stuttered.

The dishtowel hit him on the head again. And again. The more pâté that spattered off him, the harder the blows became.

'Six p.m.!'

Slowly the reality of it sank in. Herman had slept for ten hours with his head in a container of Blaashoek Pâté. In between Claire's blows he considered what had to be done.

'Enough!' he shouted. He got up, grabbed the dishtowel and yanked it out of her hands.

'We're throwing the pâté away!'

Claire leaped in front of him, like a cat who's had its tail stepped on. He recoiled, afraid that she would dig her claws into his face.

'Throw it away? Throw it *away*? Are you out of your mind?'

'But it's—'

'We're not throwing anything away, mister,' she hissed. 'You are going to finish making that pâté. Tomorrow that container will be in the deli counter as usual.' She pointed in the direction of the shop. 'And tomorrow the customers will buy it.'

'It's ruined. It would be irresponsible to—'

'It's your own fault! *You're* irresponsible! And we can't have any more of this strange behavior, Herman. You're like a walking corpse lately. I'm fed up. I'm not going to let it destroy you!'

'Hey Ma, not so loud, I could hear you all the way outside.'

They both turned. Wesley stood in the doorway panting, his face as red as his father's.

'You finish that pâté, and tomorrow we open the shop as if nothing happened,' Claire snarled. She turned and walked out the door.

Herman looked at his son.

'Lookin' good, Pa,' Wesley chuckled. Herman shrugged his shoulders.

His son slipped out of sight, but returned a few seconds later.

'Pa, I need a new bike. This city-bike is crap.'

Herman threw the dishtowel through the doorway. Wesley ducked.

'Nincompoop!' Herman spluttered. He trembled, not out of anger over his snoozing in the pâté, not out of fury over Claire's harshness; his muscles tensed into a painful cramp of disillusionment because *he could still hear them*. He had not been liberated one iota, the horror had not passed. Tonight the relentless humming would again prevent him from sleeping. He couldn't very well sleep on a mattress in the butcher shop? Claire would have him committed. And what was he to do with that pâté? Did no one commiserate with him?

He went into the hall and shouted: 'You learn to ride on an old bike, my boy!'

He sighed. He was slowly going insane. If he wasn't already.

◆

Catherine looked at the envelope, then at the mailbox, and hesitated. It was already past five o'clock, the next collection was only tomorrow morning. What if she … ? No, she couldn't just deliver it herself, she did not want to be seen there too often. Was it a good idea to post the letter at all?

Of course not. It was a terrible idea. But that's just how it is when you're in love. You do foolish things. Out of excitement. Because the nerves will eat away at your stomach lining if you don't.

So she closed her eyes and posted the letter. Back at the wheel of her car she giggled. Then she thought: what have I done? And she giggled again.

◆

After eating an omelet with bread—a suitable stand-in for herbed farmer's sausage—Saskia took out a sheet of paper and a blue felt-tip pen. She trembled slightly as she began, but ten minutes later, there it was: *I am worth just as much as anyone else.* The space between *worth* and *just* was too big, and it wasn't as elegant as she had intended. But even so, she held the sheet proudly before her. Was it crazy to hang the saying above her bed? Would people think it ridiculous? But who'd be in her bedroom, anyway? Dorien, at most, if she came by for a routine check.

She felt a vague warmth at the idea of admitting someone to her bedroom. It quickly made way for intense shame.

'Zeppos!' The dog came skipping over. 'What do you think?'

Zeppos barked.

'Do you like it?'

Saskia got up and went to the bedroom, Zeppos panting behind her. She squatted on the bed.

'Tell me if it's straight, okay Zep?'

She nervously took two thumbtacks from the nightstand. Bienvenue's roaring laugh made her drop them. Zeppos jumped, barking, from the bed.

'Shhh, Zep!'

Bienvenue's voice carried distinctly through the open window. The persistently oppressive, sultry heat seemed unlikely to let up before nightfall.

She assumed Bienvenue was looking at the turbines along the canal. One of them was very close by, just beyond the wall of their courtyard. It was huge. She had to look up in order to see the blades. It was impressive. It dominated the landscape. It protected her. She smiled.

Saskia slid onto the floor and began groping under the bed for the thumbtacks. One of them had rolled just a bit too far, she grazed her shoulder on the bedframe as she reached for it. It didn't help much that Zeppos was busy licking her heels.

She climbed, flushed, back onto the bed.

'There,' she said, and a minute later the saying hung on the wall. Not entirely straight, but straight enough. I am worth just as much as anyone else. Tomorrow she would do her best to prove it.

◆

Batman, now *he* would have a chance with Machteld. Any woman would surely fall for the six-pack in the tight black suit, the deep voice and, most of all, the awesome Batmobile. Wes saw the credits roll up the computer screen, in the direction of the Batman poster on the wall, and lay down on his bed.

Batman was a hero. And what was he? The nondescript son of a butcher. Tendency to corpulence. With a bike made of reinforced concrete. And pain. Pain everywhere. Pain in his muscles from the bike ride into the city. His legs, back, and arms were killing him, his entire body was broken. All for nothing, because Machteld did not show her face. Wes banged the mattress with his fist and then folded his hands on his belly. It felt sticky. Why didn't she turn up? Why couldn't he, for once, just get lucky?

The music and credits faded out. Now he heard the hubbub more clearly, the short, punchy sentences his mother used to browbeat his father. Dad, the ghost. Dad, with his head full of pâté. Dad, who so wanted him to take over the business. He could just put that out of his fat head. The butcher shop did not fit into Wes's future plans. He had to become more Batman, less Bracke.

He turned over. His muscles protested. His mother's harangue continued. She listed every mistake, one by one, his father had ever had the nerve to make. He sat up and the bottom sheet, which had glued itself to his skin, pulled loose. He went to the window. The pond at the back of the yard was covered with green slime. He wondered if there was even any water left, what with the dryness these past few days. Yet something else his mother could blame his father for.

The turbines glistened in the sunlight. The blades swung lethargically downwards: even they were suffering from the heat. He listened. He did not hear any hum. No whirr, no drone. Only his mother, and every so often, for a second, his father. With every downward swing of a blade, his mother's voice peaked in volume.

Now.

Now.

Now.

As though the turbines kept time with her wrath.

3

Wednesday

Magda's eyes crept across Claire's body like brown spiders. Claire's dress was partly obscured by her apron, but she could tell it was new. It suited her, drew attention away from her fat backside, although the apron mercilessly accentuated her blubber-belly. Claire smiled at Magda, greedy for her money.

'What'll it be, Magda?' The smile of a serial poisoner.

Why today, of all days, did she have to be tending the shop? Where was Herman? With a sigh Magda eyed the container of summer pâté. It lay there provocatively between the Beauvoorde pâté and the chopped liver. The moment she saw it, one second after entering the butcher shop, her nose curled in chagrin.

Everything in the shop looked normal, as it did the previous week, when Herman hadn't yet started carrying on like a crazed alcoholic. It was a prank, the butcher was testing her, they granted her just one minute of glory and then put her ruthlessly back in her place.

'How about a slice of summer pâté. As usual.'

Claire sliced off a generous slab.

'Freshly made,' Claire said. 'You'll just love it.'

The corners of Magda's mouth went up and she bared her teeth.

She wanted to see Herman. She wanted to know what state he was in. Was he lying in bed with a hangover? Was that why Claire was minding the shop? But then who had stuffed the sausages? And made the pâté? Herman was always quick to boast that only *he* knew the recipe.

'Anything else?'

'Two hamburgers,' Magda snapped.

Claire sauntered over to the opposite end of the counter. That dress really did wonders for her butt. When she wore jeans it looked like the back end of a hippopotamus. Magda chuckled to herself. Then Wesley appeared at the shop window, with the bicycle she saw him struggling with yesterday. Claire waved to him. He pretended not to see her.

'Wesley's getting athletic,' Magda said.

Claire laughed. 'He's got it into his head to cycle thirty kilometers a day. I wonder how he'll keep it up.' She put the hamburgers on the scale. 'There must be a girl in the picture, heh?' She winked. Shivers went down Magda's spine, as though Claire had just pushed her tongue into Magda's mouth.

◆

Wes had planned his excursion just before lunchtime, so that he didn't have to face his parents. He was not in the mood for hostile looks just because he no longer put cold cuts on his bread. He was also not in the mood to serve up a cliché about his sudden concern for animal welfare, or debate the ecological footprint of meat consumption. This would only earn him bitter mockery from his mother and the silent head-shaking of his father. He knew them well enough. Besides, his vegetarianism was purely pragmatic, there was no reason to pretend otherwise: eating meat was one of the two obstacles to establishing a relationship with Machteld. As the son of a butcher, he would only have a chance with the vegetarian goddess if he distanced himself from the contemptible animal abuse of Herman's Quality Meats. And how more convincingly could he prove his disgust than by banning meat from his diet? The fact that Wes chose Machteld's lifestyle above that of his own family would prove his love to her once and for all. Girls fell for boys who burned bridges and broke with their families in the name of love.

The second obstacle–the physical distance between him and his beloved–he had already neatly swept aside. He smiled to himself at the thought that his parents had so naively bought his story about the bike trips. Still, that clunky bike irritated him no end. He planned to go to the bicycle shop this afternoon, maybe he could trade in this pre-war ironwork for something more sporty, so that he no longer looked like a wanked-senseless lobster when he finally spotted her in town.

He felt his mother leering at him through the window. He ignored her. He threw his left leg over the bike and grimaced from the searing pain in his tortured muscles and joints. His untrained body had still not processed yesterday's bike ride. He hoped the pain would be worth it. He was prepared to suffer for the love of his life, but it had better be rewarded. He did not pedal all those kilometers to the city, like yesterday, just to watch old people drinking coffee at an outdoor café.

Warehouse attendant. Team leader. Night-shift laborer. Buyer. Maintenance technician.

Nothing that Saskia was qualified for. She peered through the window. Inside they had more job openings, but she didn't yet dare to take that step. First she went by all the employment offices to check the ads posted in the window. These were mostly male professions: electrician, lathe operator, personnel manager. Saskia was looking for: managerial secretary (preferably), administrative clerk (willingly), sales assistant (if necessary) or workwoman (if all else failed).

Dorien encouraged her to persevere. After nodding her way through Severine Baes's rejection letter, she slipped it, smiling, into Saskia's file.

This was how things worked, Dorien had explained. There was no need to feel unworthy or unwanted. Businesses received hundreds of applications for a single job. The odds of them choosing you were smaller than of being run over by a garbage truck in broad daylight. Saskia had to laugh at that. Since then she caught herself keeping an eye out for garbage trucks when crossing the street.

She mustn't be too picky, Dorien kept telling her. The higher her hopes, the slimmer her chances. But Dorien hadn't grown up on a farm where there was practically round-the-clock activity. Saskia wanted something new, she wanted something more distinguished than the purely physical labor from which she had fled. She pictured herself at a desk, with a computer and a printer, and a framed photo of Zep, if the boss allowed it. Of course he would allow it, she would work for a decent boss, a boss who said good morning when he came in and would grunt approvingly when he read her reports. Someone who would bring her flowers on her birthday. Now that was a dream boss!

There was nothing in this window that appealed to her. Maybe the next one. Off to the right an ad caught her eye on which she vaguely recognized the word 'secretary', and she secretly hoped the entire window would be full of tempting job vacancies. Then a car braked suddenly behind her.

It braked just like when he returned from the abattoir.

It braked just like he hadn't sold a single cow.

She froze. Her muscles cramped, she turned her head stiffly. Yes, it was him. The dirty bumper, the barely legible license plate, the mud-caked chassis.

She was back on the farm. In the distance, pigs squealed and dogs barked. The heavy odor of the manure spoiled the air. She had difficulty breathing. She knew what was coming.

◆

Wes Bracke was dying. He squeezed the brakes of his bike. As soon as his foot touched the ground, the throbbing tension in his overheated skull eased up. Not that it was much of a relief, because a painful tingling shot through his legs. His long pants–he was too ashamed of his pale legs to wear shorts–stuck to his skin. He felt dirty, as though he'd peed in his pants. Sweat flowed itchingly down his butt crack. The heat seared his parched throat as he panted. He wiped his forehead with his T-shirt. What did it matter anymore?

He had just pedaled listlessly for an hour up and down the nearly abandoned Nieuwstraat. He should have known, early in the afternoon, at the hottest time of day.

But Machteld was surely one to leave the table quickly and head out into the afternoon sun. After all, what did vegetarians eat? Carrots, lettuce and walnuts. Can't sit chewing on them all day. He did not relish the thought of spending the rest of his life as a rabbit, but for love you had to suffer. And it was healthy, or so they said. Kept you slim and trim.

His throat burned with thirst and he was famished. He craved a hamburger and a large cola. Or a smoked sausage and half a liter of beer. Or chicken curry. Or ... his intestines groaned at the thought of food. He should have gobbled down a few slices of ham on the sly. What would Machteld think of him if his guts gurgled like a clogged drainpipe while he spoke to her?

But now he most of all needed to catch his breath. This was not how he fancied meeting Machteld.

A little further on, the logo of the bicycle shop glistened, an abstract blue line drawing that looked more like eyeglasses than a bike. He hesitated. He so wanted to trade in the bicycle, but he was afraid he'd cross an important line if he did. He knew that at his age it was normal to test limits, to challenge norms and in doing so drive your parents up the wall. In that category he racked up considerable success, what with his miserable school reports and his sudden vegetarianism, although he secretly hoped that Machteld would revert to eating meat once they were a couple. He was not surprised that he'd already managed to push things this far. His parents were prepared for their teenage son to be recalcitrant and unpredictable. He could just as well put that pattern of expectation to good use. His age was perhaps not a full-blown 'license to kill', but at the very least a license to be a pain in the ass.

Yesterday his parents yelled at each other until eleven at night. His mother then popped open a bottle of white wine and proceeded to swig it. Locked in his room—a self-imposed imprisonment—he realized that this fight was different from the others. The mood had hardened; all the oxygen had been sucked out of the air, feeding the storm that had been hanging over his parents' heads for some time now. Wesley realized that the bitter atmosphere had once again narrowed his boundaries. He did not want to become the lightning rod for the negative electricity that shot between his parents. So he was better off keeping the bike for now. Moreover, his father's words kept ringing in his head: *you learn to ride on an old bike.*

He wiped his forehead with his T-shirt again, put his foot back on the pedal and groaned as his butt hit the saddle. He passed the bicycle shop, and rather than turning onto the sidewalk he swerved to the left slightly, as though to keep his distance, when a car veered alongside him.

He was nearly thrown to the ground. The old Mercedes, its green chassis obscured by dry, flaky mud, slammed on its brakes, its tires scraping against the curb. The prick at the wheel, a burly old geezer, leapt out of the car and ran, cursing, at a girl who stood reading the ads at the window of an employment agency. Wes observed the scene with nonplussed detachment. The man grabbed the girl by the throat, threw her against the shop window and flung her into the doorway.

As the man wrestled the girl along the sidewalk, Wes realized he could not simply remain an onlooker. He could abscond from the battlefield as a coward. He could film the scene on his phone and upload it to YouTube.

But he could also be a hero. In the second before he placed his foot on the pedal, he made his choice: hero. He maneuvered his bicycle onto the sidewalk and noted with satisfaction that he was soon going at quite a clip. His muscle pain had disappeared.

◆

'Traitor, stupid cow!'

Saskia heard the car door slam, the sign that it was time for her to run for it. But her legs would not move, they were riveted to the paving tiles with metal spikes. She tensed herself, not to resist, but to absorb the blows. The first punch was his smell.

'There you are, you dirty city-slut!' The hand hit her in the neck like a coal shovel and threw her against the shop window. She realized the reflex of protecting her face with her arms was a mistake. They only served as handgrips with which he slammed her into the mailboxes in the doorway. She curled up in pain, but did not fight back. Her first concern was that the mailboxes hadn't been damaged. She had no time to worry about this, because she was lifted up and dragged across the sidewalk.

'You should be ashamed, ungrateful hussy!'

'I'm sorry, Granddad,' she wanted to say. But all that came out of her mouth was a whisper, the peep of a choked mouse. She bashed against the car, chunks of mud flew off.

'I only wanted a different life,' she tried to say, but all that came out was an asthmatic pant. He pulled her up by her ponytail, against his body. She smelled the underwear she had washed so often, not the detergent but the vile stench before it went into the bucket.

'D'you understand what you're doing to me and your grandma? Who've taken such good care of you? You're just like your mother. Just. Like. Your. Mo-ther!' Each syllable was accompanied by a smack.

◆

It was a matter of meters and a matter of aiming. Most of all it was a matter of not thinking, but acting. If he thought about it too much he would hesitate or lose speed. So Wes followed his instinct. 'It's how Batman would do it,' shot through his mind. The bastard yanked the girl up against him by her ponytail. She was hunched over, leaving his left flank unprotected. He chose a single point, the hip, and focused. Two more pumps. He held his breath, felt his muscles tense.

In his gusto to slap that poor girl senseless, the old bastard didn't see him coming. Wes concentrated on the threadbare corduroy trousers. As much as he braced himself for the impact, it still came as a surprise. The old guy's hip jerked to the side, along with the handlebars. The collision shook Wes's flesh from his bones. He flew over the handlebars, against the man's chest. The old man fell backward with a scream, his ribcage breaking his fall. Wes did a somersault and landed on the employment agency's doorstep.

When he looked up, Wes saw the old man wrestling helplessly with the bike, like a soldier trying to crawl out from under his comrade's dead body. He growled and sputtered. Further up, cowering against the car door, was the girl. She was crying.

Wes waved at her. Go away, he was trying to say. Go on, run for it! But she just sat there. 'Run!' he shouted, his voice breaking, like a hysterical woman.

The girl scrambled upright. She grabbed a cloth bag off the ground and started running. Finally.

Wes leaned back. The front wheel of the bicycle, bent halfway, looked skywards. The man under it had stopped moving. Wes looked at the lifeless body and realized that he had just murdered someone.

◆

Saskia had run far enough. She leaned against a wall, wiped away a string of snot with her lower arm and rummaged in her home-made bag. Her bottom-of-the-line Nokia clattered to the pavement. Only when she bent over to pick it up did she notice that the sleeve of her T-shirt was frayed. As she grabbled for the phone the breeze that blew across her back made her suspect that the entire T-shirt was torn to ribbons. She felt a new wave of tears coming on. She pulled herself together, even though she'd have liked to give in to the numbing relief of a good cry.

Twice she dialed the wrong number, and on the third try heard the ringback tone. It took some time for Dorien to answer.

'Yes, hello?'

Nothing came out. Saskia was unable to speak.

'Hello? Is anybody there?'

'Hello, I ...' Saskia tried to bring her voice under control. She swallowed, breathed deeply, and then rattled off her story in a stream of words that gushed forth as the tears had done: profusely, overwhelmingly and without logic.

'Sorry, who's speaking?' asked the voice at the other end, when Saskia, in need of a breath, suspended the rush of words.

'It's Saskia, Dorien. Saskia Maes.'

'Are you calling for Dorien Chielens?'

Saskia started.

'Yes, I thought ...'

'Dorien is on vacation, Ms. Maes. She'll be back in three weeks. Didn't she tell you?'

No, she hadn't told her.

'Oh, that Dorien, what a scatterbrain,' the woman on the other end laughed. Then, remembering Saskia's torrent of words, added seriously: 'How can I help you?'

Saskia had no desire to tell the whole story to a complete stranger. The mutual source of words and tears had dried up. She was completely exhausted.

'It's all right,' she said. 'I'll call when she gets back. In three weeks, did you say?'

'If we can do anything to help in the meantime, all you need to do is ask. That's what we're here for.'

'Thank you. Really, thanks.'

Saskia waited until the woman hung up. She looked around her. She did not recognize the houses, and the surrounding buildings were unfamiliar, as though she were an alien from another planet. She was wandering through a world which she did not understand, and which in turn did not seem to understand her. She wanted to get back to

Blaashoek, to her apartment, to Zeppos, as soon as possible. Her only safe haven. She would stay put for three weeks, until Dorien was back to help her.

◆

Ivan Camerlynck concentrated on dissolving the zinc sulfate and the citric acid in boiling distilled water. He was keyed up. Soon Mrs. Deknudt would be coming by to pick up her zinc syrup, and there was no time to lose. Making her wait for ten minutes would come across as unprofessional. So he gathered together the sugar syrup, the vanilla essence and the nipagin preservative.

Waf waf waf!

Ivan gritted his teeth. That damned dog. He added the three substances to the solution.

Waf waf!

Where was that stupid girl, actually? Lolling in bed recovering from a night's 'work'? Snoring so loudly she didn't even hear her own monster bark? Or was she just too lazy to train the animal properly?

This was the moment of truth. If he spilled or splashed, the whole process was ruined. He added just the right amount of distilled water to bring the mixture to the desired weight.

Waf waf waf!

Enough! He stormed through the kitchen at the back of the pharmacy and jerked open the sliding glass door leading to the courtyard. Heat blew onto his face. He threw a chair against the wall. The barking only got louder, a piercing, hysterical blare that infuriated Ivan even more. The animal smelled him, and growled. Ivan climbed gingerly onto the chair. He kept himself low against the dividing wall, hoping the dog would forget him. He heard paw-steps darting back and forth along the wall, the panting interrupted now and then by a gulping sound. Ivan stared behind him toward the open door. His eyes glided along the meager interior of the kitchenette to the dark opening that led to his pharmacy. He had to get back to the zinc syrup. What in God's name was he doing scrunched up against a wall, listening to a barking dog?

Waf waf waf! Waf waf waf!

Ivan pulled himself slowly upward along the wall. He peeked over it, careful not to breathe or in any way attract the animal's attention.

The dog did not notice him. It gazed upward, fixated, and howled as though an invisible evil hovered above. What was wrong with that animal? Ivan followed the direction of the snout. And then he saw the fiend that was driving the little yapper into such a frenzy.

The turbine towered above them. Every blade that swooped downwards was treated to a shrill bark. There's green energy for you, Ivan thought. There's the benefit that modern times had brought to Blaashoek. This hadn't occurred to them, did it, all those clever engineers. They made off with their thousands of euros' worth of studies and spreadsheets, and left the people of Blaashoek in the lurch. Did they give a damn that he was being driven bonkers by a frightened dog? Did they give a damn that those rotten turbines were ruining his life? No, sir! They hadn't a clue, those smart alecks, and if they did know, they pretended not to. Mister Ivan should be grateful that his humble dwelling was now being powered by green energy. Well, Mister Ivan was *not* grateful!

Waf waf waf!

'Quiet!'

He did not shout it, he hissed it. The dog lost interest in the turbines. Growling, he approached Ivan and barked threateningly.

'Shut your trap!'

The dog skittered back a meter and then leapt forward.

Waf waf waf waf waf waf waf!

'Shut it, you damned mongrel!'

Ivan clenched the wall in anger, as though it were the dog's throat. But the creature did not stop barking.

'Shhht! Ksssst!'

Waf waf waf!

'Cur! Be quiet, damn you!'

Could he bash the mutt's brains in? No, no blunt objects at hand. He sighed, stood up straight and peered through the apartment's back window. There was no movement; the modern kitchen—far more expensive than his—was neat but bare, even deathly so. The curtains were drawn on the other downstairs window. That silly cow lay there sound asleep, or else she had gone out. His gaze continued upward along the back wall.

In the window of the upstairs apartment stood a naked woman. He got a glimpse of her voluptuous body—she had a narrow waist and firm breasts with large nipples—before she disappeared from view.

He forgot all about the dog. Ivan climbed down from the chair, his legs trembling. He looked back up at the window, but it was empty, as if the nude woman had been a figment of his imagination. He hadn't seen her face. But what a body! What a damned sexy body!

His heart pounded in his throat. He stared back at the window. She didn't reappear. Had she got as big a shock as he did? Nothing like this had ever happened to him before. Then a chill came over him. Was it that hussy from downstairs, the owner of the yapping dog? Impossible. How could such a gorgeous body be concealed under that ratty T-shirt and cheap jeans? Miracles never cease, he thought, but this was too good to be true.

He had seen a woman upstairs. In the black man's house. Ivan massaged his chin and rubbed the side of his nose, as though he were deliberating the composition of a certain medication. Who was it? Ivan went into the pharmacy and leaned on the counter, like he did when explaining the daily dosage of a drug to a customer. He looked at the rack of suntan products, thought of Mrs. Deknudt's medicine, and then in his mind he saw that naked woman at the window again. She had the body of a model. She was naked because she had been fucking.

How did he do it? How did he manage to snag such a beautiful woman? He hardly spoke the language, officially was dead broke, and his chances on the job market were about as good as a one-armed sexagenarian. Was she a drug addict who paid the Negro with her body?

Ivan shook the thought out of his head. As plausible as it sounded, the body was stylish, and she stood at the window as though she were posing for a photo shoot. Not for just any old skin mag, but for *Playboy* or a black-and-white calendar on glossy paper: 'tastefully nude', they called it. A heroin whore did not have that kind of class.

Ivan sighed. He wanted to see her again. He wanted to see her standing at his own window. But he knew that his dream was just that: a utopian fantasy. As an upright, hard-working pharmacist he didn't stand a chance with this kind of woman, who by an unfortunate trick of nature was invariably attracted to brutish and callous men, men from the wrong side of the tracks who brought them to grief, drink and drugs.

Ivan paced back to the kitchenette. He had to lean all the way over the sink in order to have a view of the neighboring window. From here the only thing he could see was the reflection of the turbine. He cursed. He opened the sliding door, ignored the frantic barking, and stared upward, but now all he saw was a vague reflection and a bit of ceiling. There was no point, she was gone.

When she left the house, he realized with a jolt, she would have to pass the pharmacy. He raced back through the kitchen and the pharmacy, and installed himself behind the rack of suntan products. Not a soul. The asphalt shimmered like molten tar that swallowed you the moment you set foot on it. The hot goo would wrap itself in sticky coils around your ankles; the next day you would read in the papers how you had been freed by the fire department and that the government had slapped you with a million-euro claim for damaging public property.

The woman was nowhere to be seen. She did not sink to her ankles in the syrupy asphalt, she did not parade naked past his shop window. She did not even trot elegantly across the street. Ivan sighed and realized suddenly that the zinc syrup was still waiting. Mrs. Deknudt could show up any moment now, and the zinc syrup had to be as good as the salve for Farmer Pouseele's wife.

◆

'He saw me,' Catherine screeched. She sprang back, banged into the edge of the bed and fell backward onto the mattress. She lay there for a moment, savoring his scent and her scent—their scent—then swung across the bed and skipped to the bathroom.

'He saw me, *il m'a vue*,' she said to the shower curtain, behind which Bienvenue's silhouette moved.

'Who saw you?' he asked, loud and songlike, with that dark voice that made her legs turn to jelly.

'Camerlynck,' she replied. 'He saw me at the window.'

'Camerlynck, *c'est qui?*'

'The pharmacist, your next-door neighbor. He saw me standing there stark naked, *toute nue*.'

She slid the curtain aside, looked at his exquisite ass and then at his robust head, which tried to look at her over his shoulder. He turned around.

'Il m'a vue toute nue,' she repeated and thrust her bosom forward.

Bienvenue laughed and turned off the water. She handed him a towel and stepped aside to let him pass. He dried himself hastily, went over to the window and stood there, naked.

'Where is he?'

She looked over his shoulder.

'He's gone. He was looking over the wall, yelling at the dog.'

Bienvenue laughed again.

'Why yell at the dog? Does the dog understand Dutch?'

'Better than you do.'

Bienvenue grabbed her by her waist and threw her onto the bed. With an agile leap he was next to her, and before she knew it they were intertwined.

'No, Bienvenue, not now, I haven't got time.' She regretted having come here after all. The letter had been mailed yesterday—she hadn't mentioned it, it was to be a surprise. But why couldn't she control herself? What made her park the car up the street, as usual, and sneak into the house like a burglar? Why was she lying in his bed yet again? She pushed him off her.

'Sorry, Bienvenue, I really have to go. And besides, we've just showered.'

'Il nous reste encore du temps.'

She sighed. She stared through the window at the turbine. The rhythmic sweep of the blades had something comforting to it. Bienvenue touched her breasts. She turned and placed her index finger on his mouth.

'Silence, Bienvenue.' She smiled and ran her hand over his

face. His own hand slid over her belly, she knew exactly where that hand was headed, so she brushed it aside. She jumped out of bed, quickly pulled on her panties and snatched her bra and dress from the floor.

'Ah, Catherine ...'

If she didn't get dressed *tout de suite* she'd soon let him seduce her again. But Catherine couldn't stay. That pharmacist, she couldn't get him out of her head. She skipped into the living room and stepped into her shoes. He followed her and put his arms around her. She laid her head against his chest.

'I have to go.' She looked up at him. 'Tomorrow you'll get a surprise from me.'

His face cleared, which made her smile.

She kissed him, opened the door, waved once more, and off she went.

◆

Herman Bracke showed the salesman out—his pushy sales pitch about the newest developments in deli packaging paper had given him a throbbing headache—when a police car stopped right in front of the butcher shop. Through the shop window he saw Claire look worriedly at the eye-catching vehicle. She was scooping crab salad into a plastic container. Her movements froze when the two police officers helped an awkward teenage boy out of the car. Their son. He hung his head like a sex offender caught red-handed. To make matters worse, all the customers in the shop stared along with her.

Herman's headache pounded even harder. He had to see the salesman off as quickly as possible, but as he led him toward his car the man turned and gawked, waiting for the spectacle to play out.

'Thanks again for your expert demonstration,' Herman

ventured, as the police escorted Wesley into the shop. 'I'll be in touch.'

'Hm, hm,' the man nodded. With a smirk he turned to Herman. 'Had a break-in?'

Herman did not know what he was getting at. He only wanted to be rid of him, and the headache. The man pointed to the butcher shop, where customers, conversing animatedly, filed out the door. 'Well, if you've been robbed, it looks like they've nabbed the culprit.' He put on his sunglasses and grinned. Perhaps he grinned the same way when he plopped into the driver's seat of his company car with a signed contract.

'Yes, I'll go have a look.' He shook the salesman's hand. 'Thanks again.' He hurried back to the now-empty butcher shop, an awful sensation on a day that begged for a barbecue—the sausages, merguez, ribs, kebabs, and chicken legs lay stacked in the cooler. Claire had already led the police officers to the living room. He closed the door and rolled down the blinds. To his chagrin the salesman was still hanging around at the curb, as though he hoped this might just be his lucky day.

The container of Blaashoek Pâté was three-quarters empty. A fleeting smile passed over Herman's lips. Once again, Claire was right. Before he opened the door to the living room he knew this would be his single happy moment of the day, and that his headache would only get worse. The police officers got up from the sofa when he entered. His son sat hangdog in an armchair and Claire sniffled on the other side of the coffee table.

'Afternoon, Mr. Bracke,' said the senior of the two, a friendly-looking man. 'Officers Hauspie and Huyghe.' He pointed to himself and his colleague, a young, attractive woman. Her open, charming face gave him hope that it wouldn't be such bad news after all.

'What's going on?' he asked. He looked over at Wesley, who stared stubbornly at his feet. Claire raised her head and then let it droop back into her handkerchief.

'Your son was involved in an incident this afternoon,' Officer Hauspie said. He paused, as though to add dramatic tension.

'An incident?'

'Your son rode into a man in town.'

'Rode into someone? The boy doesn't even have a driver's license!' Herman laughed. They had obviously picked up the wrong person.

'With his bicycle, Mr. Bracke.'

Herman said nothing. He would continue to do so for a while longer. Wesley ride into someone with his bike? What possessed him? So it was true what they said about your brain cells dying off when you don't eat meat. But so soon?

'We haven't established the details yet, as there are some discrepancies between the accounts of your son and the man he hit. According to your son, the man was harassing a girl. He wanted to help and all he could think of was to ram into the man with his bicycle.'

He paused again. Wesley glanced up, and then returned to studying the pattern on the rug. The rug had been a gift from Herman's sister. He thought it was ugly. As though she read his mind, Claire shrugged her shoulders: this was not the time to start carping about the rug.

'There were no eyewitnesses, so corroborating the accounts won't be easy. Right now we're most interested in talking to the girl.'

The officers got up, as though they expected the girl to leap out of a cupboard. When that did not happen, they made moves to take their leave.

'And now?' Herman asked.

Officer Hauspie raised his palms in the air.

'Your son can stay at home. When we've completed our investigation, the prosecutor will decide whether he has to appear in juvenile court. Tomorrow you have an appointment with the court's social services.' He walked through to the butcher shop, Herman dragging along behind him, and peered at the sausages behind the glass counter. Perhaps he had missed his midday meal thanks to a teenager with delusions of heroism.

'Would you care for a few sausages?' Herman asked. 'On the house.'

Officer Hauspie turned to him and grinned.

'Thank you, Mr. Bracke. Our salary isn't all that impressive, but not so bad that we can't afford our own dinner.'

All of Herman's blood rushed to his head and made his legs weak.

'I didn't mean ... I just wanted to ...' He was better off keeping quiet. He fumbled with the lock on the door, which always seemed to stick at moments like this. He finally got it open, and, still blushing, led the police officers outside. The salesman was gone, Herman noted with relief.

'The man your son rode into hasn't taken legal action yet. Not yet. But I wouldn't be surprised if he does,' said Hauspie while Huyghe headed for the squad car. 'He's in the hospital. Dislocated hip, bruised and broken ribs, perforated liver. Not a pretty sight. Right now he's got other things on his mind than lawsuits. But once he's over the worst part, you're in for it, I'm afraid.'

Herman nodded.

'It all really depends on the girl's account. We have an idea who it is. We'll keep you posted.'

He gave Herman a firm handshake.

'Mr. Bracke, I wish you a good day, in spite of all this.'

Herman nodded. A good day: he wondered if he would ever experience that again.

◆

If she had known, Magda would have smashed the plate to smithereens on Walter's head when he got home. Having just set the table for his afternoon tea, she missed the arrival of the police car in front of the butcher shop. Even though a squad car was not spectacular in itself, the simple presence of the police would rekindle her hope that, after all, there *was* something amiss, that not everything was back to normal, that the demise of Herman's butcher shop had been accelerated beyond expectation.

But now she was standing at the kitchen table, arranging fork, knife, summer pâté, butter and newspaper for her mailman. In passing she skimmed the headlines—some to-do about asylum seekers holed up in a church, a TV presenter and her premature baby and a blunder by the Ministry of Finance—as she unwrapped the wax paper from the pâté and cut off a slice. She tasted it with the same reservation as a five-star chef would test an hors d'oeuvre prepared by an apprentice. It tasted the same as always, perhaps a bit more sour. She cut off another slice. It was good; in fact, it was outstanding. Herman Bracke was simply a champion when it came to pâté.

Pity you didn't realize these things when you're seventeen. What would Herman Bracke have looked like as a seventeen-year-old? Like Wesley? Maybe even more of a dopey fatso, she thought. She wouldn't have given him the time of day. She fell for a well-toned physique with a head of black curls, an amusing, athletic type who turned somersaults in the waves, who always won at beach volleyball, who gave her lifts on the back of his bike whenever he organized a picnic. An outgoing boy who made friends easily, a dreamer who spent more time on protest marches and demonstrations than on his studies, a boy straight out of a TV series, which made him even more butch and attractive. It was a pity, she thought, that she had made her partner choice before she had to worry about supporting herself, and therefore applied the wrong criteria: a washboard stomach, popularity, sex appeal.

While Herman, averse to female attentions, focused on his future and a well-filled bank account, her popular Walter muddled along, and succeeded in squandering both her and his future, not only by getting her pregnant, but also in eschewing higher education and embracing the life of a simple laborer, which according to Walter was far nobler than the environmentally damaging and unethical business world. With his postman's salary they were condemned to a life of bank loans, second-hand cars, domestic vacations and shopping at budget stores.

If only she could start all over again. She sliced off another piece of pâté. Now it really did have a sour bite. But that could just be her.

◆

Catherine already heard the shots as she turned off the engine of the 207CC. She sighed, got out of the car and opened the door to the house. Whenever she came inside on a hot summer day, she enjoyed the coolness of the front hall. She walked through the living room and stood at the sliding glass doors, looking out into the backyard, where the turbine blades threw long shadows across the grass. What was Jan's problem? She wasn't bothered by the shadows; on the contrary, if she looked at them for long enough, those serenely sweeping smudges rocked her to sleep. She imagined how marvelous it would be to live here with Bienvenue. No more grousing about a dominant mother who showed up every week at an inopportune moment, no more childish grumbling about the assault on the backyard. Bienvenue would not complain about the yard, he would lead Catherine to the softest patch of grass and fuck her to the rhythm of the blades.

She slid open the door and the heat hit her squarely in the face. A tin can caught the bullet with a metallic *tock*, a gruesome death rattle. She shivered. She wandered into the yard and stopped under the swooping shadows. She had been a fool today. Yesterday she had posted the letter telling Bienvenue she needed some breathing space. Otherwise she would become totally addicted to him. The more she went to see him, the sooner she wanted to return. And each time she yielded to her desire, she was taking an enormous risk. Secrets were impossible to keep in a town like this. It was already a minor miracle that no one had spilled the beans to Jan yet. Maybe her salvation lay in the age-old cliché that the cuckolded partner is the last one to find out.

Yesterday, when she left the apartment, she bumped into the girl she'd seen with the dog in Jan's practice the day before. When she nearly stumbled over her, she decided once and for all to cool it with Bienvenue. In her letter she explained that he would not see her for at least a week, had enclosed a small gift, and posted it after buying the barbecue meat and charcoal briquettes. And now, not even twenty-four hours after stating her rock-solid resolution, and genuinely believing in it herself, she had his taste in her mouth and his scent on her body, a scent she hoped only she could smell.

Still, that was not what vexed her the most. Her disquiet materialized in that one split second, just before she leapt back from the window, when Camerlynck's gaze passed over her body. Despite the sizzling midday heat she shivered at the thought of that creep, how he leered over the garden wall like an idiot and screamed at the downstairs girl's dog. How he, as though on cue, looked up the back wall and spotted her. She hoped he did not recognize her, that he'd been too distracted by the unexpected sight of female nudity to look at her face.

While she could invent any number of excuses to explain the encounter with the girl, the confrontation with Camerlynck was impossible to shrug off. No two ways about it: she stood naked in Bienvenue's window. And if Camerlynck had recognized her, it wouldn't be long before the rest of the town knew too. Her skin tautened in goosebumps and a chill ran down her back like an ice cube, and it was not because of the bang of another tin can being ripped open.

◆

Her back was covered in red welts. Under her armpit they fanned out into purply-blue blotches that hurt when she touched them. It had been at least six months since she had felt this. Saskia knew how her injured body would keep her awake at night, how the blueish-purple bruises would evolve to greenish-brown and then to yellow. Even an hour in the shower wasn't enough to wash off all the anguish.

The T-shirt was now ready for the rag basket. She was sorry about that, it was her favorite. She took one of her other two T-shirts from the cupboard and winced as she pulled it over her head. The fabric chafed like sandpaper over her wounds. No bra today; she couldn't face the torture. She sat down on the bed, slowly pulled on her trousers, concealing the welts and bruises that covered her legs like an abstract painting. She had weak veins and was susceptible to bruising.

Zeppos did figure-eights around her feet. She did not have the energy to pet him.

'Sweet Zeppos,' she whispered. 'My sweet little Zeppos.'

The doorbell rang. Zeppos pricked up his ears and charged out of the bedroom. Saskia stiffened. Granddad! Groaning, she crept under the sheets. The bell rang again. Zeppos barked.

'Come, Zep,' she whispered. She dug herself deeper into bed, shut her eyes and plugged her ears. Granddad cursed and banged on the door. Eventually he bashed it so hard it flew out of its hinges. Livid, he stormed through the apartment. She screamed.

Nothing happened. The door was sturdy, he couldn't break it down. She hoped. She hoped with all her might.

Saskia held her breath. The bell rang again, longer than the first few times. Granddad must be furious. Now she really wouldn't open up. If that door didn't hold up, her moments would be numbered. Zeppos barked. Saskia heard him trot back to the bedroom. He stood waiting at the door, panting. She did nothing. She just lay there stock-still.

The bell rang again. Zeppos raced off.

And then, nothing more.

◆

'She's not home,' Officer Huyghe said.

'Or not answering,' Hauspie sighed. He rang the bell again, longer this time.

'Ms. Maes, police,' he called to the door. He bent over to shout something through the letter slot.

'Come on, let's go, there's no point,' Huyghe said. Hauspie waited at the door for another two minutes until finally giving up.

◆

While his parents were busy upbraiding each other in the living room—strange, considering *he* was the guilty party—Wes scoured the news sites in search of accounts of his heroic feat. Apparently the outside world was not impressed either at the way he had saved a girl's life that afternoon. Now he understood how Batman felt when he had been declared a public enemy of the city he tried to protect. Did he really expect a ticker-tape parade for his deed? Well, yes, in fact he did. Okay, he hadn't rescued anyone from a burning house in the middle of the night, but this was no trifle either. The country was swarming with pedophiles and rapists, and now a teenage boy could finally make positive news instead of falling prey to drugs or truancy or whatever all those old farts thought was so shocking about today's youth. But no, not a word. Would they rather have seen the girl pummeled, punted and raped? And dumped in the doorway?

He was about to give up his internet search when he was struck by the brainwave of surfing to the site of the local newspaper. It was an act of desperation. And there it was, not too big but still visible, in the column of short items on the right-hand side, with the headline: 'Incident with bicycle'.

He clicked on it.

> This afternoon, a strange incident took place in front of the employment agency on the Nieuwstraat. Around midday a cyclist rode into an elderly man, who was seriously injured in his hip and ribs. The cyclist, a young man of approximately seventeen, was taken to the police station for questioning and later released. According to police sources, the young man, who has no previous criminal record, asserted that the elderly man had been harassing a girl. The police were as yet unable to comment

on this account. A failed robbery attempt has not been discounted.

Wes reread the item. Criminal record! Attempted robbery! They were making him out to be the culprit, damn it. Was the girl worth all this trouble?

He knew well enough that he had saved her not only because he was such a righteous goody two-shoes. He had done it mostly to make an impression. On Machteld, in the end.

That is why he clicked on the 'share' icon, chose the social network site, and posted the item with the heading 'Girl rescued this afternoon on the Nieuwstraat'. How his 351 friends would react did not interest him. It was all about her. About Machteld.

4

Thursday

At 2 a.m. Dr. Jan Lietaer was sitting on the toilet. He groaned as his diarrhea splashed into the bowl with such force that he felt it spatter back up against his buttocks. Not only his guts but also his stomach constricted, so that he endured a simultaneous stream of shit from one end and sour gall from the other. Jan needed nearly half a roll of toilet paper to clean his backside, and when he finally went to pull up his underpants he felt a new wave pushing against his sphincter.

Jan Lietaer was not alone that night. There were many others. Across town, for instance, Walter and Magda De Gryse took turns cursing while on the crapper (Magda swore much louder than Walter, who in turn had more frequent cramps). In the ramshackle townhouse across from the pharmacy, old Mrs. Deknudt's knees were too weak to get her to the bathroom in time. She collapsed on the floor in the middle of the hallway, and was forced to let it all out onto the expensive art-deco tiles, which she noticed, now being so close by, could use a mopping. She really should get a housekeeper; she was getting too old to keep the place up all by herself. Tomorrow she would call a cleaning service. If, at least, she survived this torment. For although Mrs. Deknudt had seen her share of hardship—during the war she had eaten tulip bulbs and sugar beets—she genuinely believed her last hour had struck.

◆

The cramp took him by surprise a good kilometer outside Blaashoek. Walter thought he would make it home, but he was mistaken. It was now too late for regrets. 'Stay home,' Magda had shouted to him through the bathroom door. 'Stay home and call in sick.' That word alone—'sick'—made him decide to go to work after all, even though his eyelids drooped with fatigue, and his insides felt like a lottery ball machine. 'I haven't called in sick a day in my life, and I'm not about to do it today,' he wanted to say, but he did not dare: contradicting Magda was to sign your own death warrant. Besides, a sudden cramp took his breath away.

He had to concentrate on something else, otherwise he wouldn't be able to hold it in any longer. Just one more kilometer, and once he got home he could race to the—

Too late. He lifted his butt from the bike saddle, but could not prevent his sphincter from opening just a tad. A warm dampness crept up his crack and clung coolly to his skin. Walter cursed. Wobbling, he steered the bicycle onto the shoulder, jumped off and slid down the bank to the canal. He hoped the turbines would be the only witnesses.

Soon enough he noticed three recreational boats moored at the water's edge. There was no turning back. All the way down the bank, his body looked forward to the release. His sphincter loosened, his intestines prepared to push. He squatted and, before he knew it, he saw the sludge run between his feet and down the brownish grass.

Oh, the relief. Despite the awkward position and the fear of soiling his uniform, the first seconds were liberating. That delicious moment of release blocked out the embarrassing gurgle of his guts and the raucous farts that went with it. Walter tried not to look at the shit, but could not resist stealing the occasional glance at the brown river that snaked under his trousers and down the bank. He focused on a nearby patch of buttercups. They swayed in the gentle breeze, as though nodding at him approvingly: well done, Walter, there was no holding it in any longer. And if you can't hold it in, why not just let it all hang out? He chuckled and turned his attention to the yachts, and then to the turbines. With one last death rattle the squirts came to an end, for now at least. Walter sighed and tried to stand up.

Then, feeling a second wave coming on, he braced himself. Again he fixed his gaze on the buttercups. This time they did not wave so encouragingly.

The sloshing of the water against the yachts was soothing. He should come back here sometime, just to enjoy the nature in the shadow of the turbines. The yacht nearest him, he noticed, was called *Egoist*. What an awful name. How could people with so much money have such total lack of good taste? All right, that they drove an x5 or a Cayenne, he could stomach: everyone had the right to want to compensate for a certain shortcoming. That they wore pink dress shirts with white collars, fine, it was entirely up to them if they wanted to dress like dorks. But name your boat 'Egoist'? That was the epitome of decadence.

Just under the 'g' was a porthole. Behind the porthole a small face smiled at him. The head moved. Blonde curls bobbed up and down, the little face glanced behind, and then back toward him. Now he also saw a small hand, which waved at him. The child turned around again, as though it were being spoken to. Then a man's face appeared behind the child, who had stopped smiling and waving. The man's face was gone as abruptly as it had come. The child vanished as well.

Shit! Walter quickly wiped his backside with a few clumps of grass he'd tugged out of the ground, and struggled to stand up. His legs, sluggish from all that squatting, could not support him and he slipped in the diarrhea, his trousers still down around his knees, and rolled over onto his side, crushing the buttercups. He had to pull up his pants before he could clamber back up the bank. The elastic band of his underwear got caught under his balls.

'Hey, you there!'

The Egoist spoke with a Limburg accent. Walter zipped up his fly. He began the climb to his bicycle.

'Hey, *hey*, you!'

Walter heard the man clatter over the deck of his boat, but did not dare turn to look.

'Come back here, mister!'

Walter clambered further. It was rough going. For some reason a throbbing warmth shot from his right hand to his forearm.

'I'll find you, you pervert! I'm calling the police!'

While the man continued shouting abuse, Walter wobbled into Blaashoek on his bicycle. The same pain that made both his hands tingle, he now felt itching his buttocks. His one hand was covered with red blotches and white blisters. Walter realized what he must have used to wipe his ass.

'No, no, no,' he groaned.

◆

Magda staggered to the pharmacy. She sighed with relief when she saw that there was no one in the stuffy waiting area. Nor was Mr. Camerlynck anywhere to be seen. She leaned across the counter, for she had no time to waste, and peered into the area at the back. She held her breath, afraid the pharmacist would catch her spying on him. She saw him standing in the kitchenette, he was gazing up out of the window, like a child fixated on a hot-air balloon.

She couldn't hang around waiting for Camerlynck to snap out of his reverie. She shuffled back and forth, and cleared her throat. She coughed and drummed her fingers on the glass countertop. Under it was a poster. *Get tough on fungus!* Colorful boxes of vitamin supplements were displayed on the shelves behind the counter. She drummed on the glass again, just above the little green monster that lifted up a toenail so it could nestle itself underneath. She was just about to lean over the counter again to peer through the doorway when she heard Ivan Camerlynck scuffle toward her.

'Ah, Mrs. De Gryse,' he said as he entered the shop, 'what a pleasure to see you here.' But his languid tone conveyed just the opposite: that he wished she would beat it.

Magda stared at the large yellow teeth that filled his smile, and said: 'A box of Imodium, please, Mr. Camerlynck.' She was embarrassed by the request, as usual, because she was convinced the pharmacist passed judgment on her every time he dealt with one of her prescriptions.

'Imodium,' Camerlynck mumbled. He shuffled over to a drawer lined with neatly arranged boxes. His knobbly fingers fished one out, he scanned the barcode and typed something into the computer.

'You're the third one today,' he said as Magda opened her wallet. 'Summer's just begun, hardly the time of year you'd expect a stomach virus to be going around.' He turned and smiled at her. 'Or might everyone have eaten something disagreeable yesterday?'

Magda did not answer. She was in a hurry to pay.

'Perhaps Herman's barbecue sausages were spoiled,' Camerlynck chuckled.

'Who else, then? For the Imodium?' Magda asked. Suddenly she saw a large container before her, a container that had sat there mocking her from behind a deli counter the day before. Behind that counter a fat ass flaunted a new dress.

'What's that you ask, Mrs. De Gryse?' Camerlynck sniggered, as though she had just asked for hemorrhoid cream. 'You know I can't tell you who buys what medicine. That's confidential!'

He took her money. 'But I *can* tell you I won't be needing any Imodium today.' He smiled again, and sniffed for good measure.

'I don't think it was Herman's barbecue sausages,' Magda said. 'But may I ask, Mr. Camerlynck, whether you ever eat Herman's summer pâté?'

'Of course you may ask, Mrs. De Gryse.' The pharmacist put the pills in a paper bag, ensuring Magda's medical privacy when she crossed the street. 'I never eat pâté. Maybe it's just me, but I always wonder what goes in it. Have you ever stopped to think about it? Surely a butcher doesn't grind his *best* meat into pâté?'

Magda nodded.

◆

At the very moment that Magda opened her front door, planning first to go to the bathroom, then take an Imodium pill, and after that call the local journalist, Jan Lietaer sat, bare-chested, staring out of his front window onto the street. He looked at a tree, a hedge, a parked car, at everything that fit into the frame of his front window, without consciously seeing anything. Then he stared at the blank TV screen, as though he expected the news to turn itself on automatically. He stared at the mailbox when he heard it rattle and then at the postman who cycled past his window. Walter was in a hurry today, the devil was nipping at his heels. Jan's skin itched from the perspiration. He scratched, but the itch would not go away. He rubbed his back against the upholstery of the armchair. That helped somewhat.

The warfare in his intestines appeared to have subsided, three hours after he had discovered a lone pill in the bathroom medicine cabinet. Now all he felt was empty and bored, with a dull headache behind his temples. He stared at length at the thermostat knob on the radiator, and then returned his attention to the mailbox. Should he empty it? Every fiber in his body said No. He scratched his chest hair and let his hand slide down to his navel, from which he plucked a piece of lint. He rolled the lint into a tiny cigar shape and flicked it away.

Well, he *could* go and get the mail. He sighed. First check if there was anything to dig out of his nose. Left nostril: nothing. Right one: also nothing.

He would receive no clients today. Not only because probably none would come, but also because he did not feel like it. It would be another stiflingly hot day. It was high time it rained, for the sake of his lawn. His beautiful lawn in his Provençal garden. That is what he would do, in a bit: wheel the chaise longue out back and spend the day dozing in the sun, drink the occasional cola, or beer. No shooting practice today. His exhausted mind was not up to it. He hoped the shadows of the turbine blades would not disturb his nap.

He would try to get used to it. Like it or not, that stupid turbine was a fait accompli. They weren't ever going to tear it down. Public opinion was behind it. Jan knew all too well how opposition to governmental building frenzy went. The district about to be razed to make way for an expressway always rebelled under the leadership of the neighborhood firebrand. It never helped, because the rest of the populace didn't give a damn. Anything to get them to the beach quicker in the summer. Protests were limited to that one street, and soon enough the young families moved out—the ones who could afford to, at least—until all that was left was one lone middle-aged diehard with a pathetic placard on the front of his house.

It was the same with the wind park. The city people, the ones who didn't have to look up at them every day, thought they were terrific. He could foment, protest and campaign like a Don Quixote. He had done his share of grousing and grumbling, particularly to Catherine. It didn't accomplish anything, on the contrary. So Jan decided to resign himself to it. Spineless, his mother called it. Who cares. Solitary resistance was senseless. There were plenty of other, far more enjoyable, senseless things to do.

Jan yawned. A nap would do him good. He got up from the sofa, making him go slightly dizzy. He stretched his arms, and his vertebrae clicked back into position. He sniffed his armpits. Not too bad. He shuffled to the mailbox and opened the latch. Ah, the newspaper, he had totally forgotten about it. The news of the day would be an agreeable partner on the chaise longue.

There were more letters than he'd expected. He glanced through them, and discovered two envelopes for number 27. It was not like Walter to make this kind of mistake. The last time he got a letter for 27 instead of 72, three years ago, shortly after New Year, he teased Walter for six months about it. No matter, he would bring them over to number 27 himself later. Or tomorrow, that seemed more realistic.

Now his main priority was getting out into the garden. He laid the letters on the small table next to the mailbox, skimmed the headlines on the front page of the paper—a man had taken his wife and daughter hostage, the Minister of Defense had tried to write off a junket as a business trip, and refuse had been dumped in a river—and went into the kitchen, where he took a painkiller with some water before heading out back.

◆

'There. That's where he was.' The man pointed to a spot opposite the boat. Officer Hauspie saw a vague brown stain, with flies circling above it. He did not require closer inspection to know what it was.

'Tell me exactly what happened, Mr. ...'

'De Graaff. Well, the man squatted right there, did his business and showed his genitals to my daughter.' The man pointed to a girl of about six, with adorable blonde curls. She looked up at her father as only little girls of six can. 'Go on back inside, Lara,' instructed De Graaff. The child obeyed.

'Can you describe the man?' Officer Hauspie asked.

'I didn't get a good look at his face, but I think he had dark hair.'

'You were too distracted by his other body parts,' Officer Hauspie quipped. Huyghe, standing off to the side, tried to suppress a laugh.

'I hope you're not planning to make light of this! That pervert sat there naked in front of my boat, in full view of my daughter, and you're cracking jokes? What kind of country is this? I demand a full inquiry!'

'Don't you worry, sir. What was the man wearing?'

'He was dressed totally in blue.' De Graaff shot Hauspie a threatening glance, as though to warn him against tossing in another wisecrack.

'In blue,' the policeman repeated.

'And on his T-shirt was a red and white emblem, from a distance it looked like the Tommy logo.'

'Tommy?'

'Tommy Hilfiger,' the man sighed. 'The designer.'

Officer Hauspie nodded and made a note in his memo book: *Tommy Hillfinger.*

He walked along the water's edge. De Graaff followed him. Hauspie turned and his eyes were drawn to the white giants. If he looked at them long enough, they might hypnotize him. He turned away; they made him nervous.

'You are going to take a specimen, aren't you? As evidence?'

Hauspie scrunched his nose. Not a chance. The sight alone of the humming swarm of fat flies turned his stomach.

'That won't be necessary, for the time being.'

'But that shit's full of DNA! You'll be able to identify the culprit!'

'Take it from me, we'll find him. And once we have, he'll be charged with public indecency. If you like, you can file a complaint as the injured party.' Hauspie caught himself assuming a Limburg accent, and found that he was getting awfully tired of this windbag De Graaff.

'You bet I will. Right now, if I can.'

'I'll have to ask you to come around to the station this afternoon. We've got all the necessary forms there to process your complaint.'

De Graaff made a face. 'Well, all right, I'll gladly give up my afternoon to catch that scumbag.'

'I'd like to thank you for alerting us. I'll let you know if we find him.'

'Seems to me the least you can do.' He climbed onto the deck of his boat and disappeared into the cabin. End of conversation.

Hauspie smiled at Huyghe, and let her lead the way up the bank to the street.

'Take a specimen, who's he kidding?'

'I don't think it's such a bad idea, Roger,' Huyghe laughed. Hauspie swallowed.

'As long as we're in Blaashoek anyway, why don't we pay Saskia Maes another visit,' he said.

◆

Claire nearly had a heart attack when Hauspie and Huyghe drove past the butcher shop. She was seized by visions of the patrol car stopping and her son stepping out. But that was not possible, Wesley was upstairs playing computer games while his father prepared to take him to see the juvenile court's social worker. Herman planned to wear his best suit, to make a good impression. Her panic only subsided once the police car had vanished from view.

It was surprisingly quiet in the butcher shop. Normally Mrs. Deknudt, Magda De Gryse, and Catherine Lietaer would have stopped in for meat by now. But today, no one. Rumor of Wesley's shenanigans had probably made its way along the grapevine. There were no secrets in this town. Anyone who stepped out of line got the cold shoulder. A shopkeeper who did so lost business. Misconduct was paid for in cash.

Was this her fate? That the townspeople would shun the butcher shop because their son had become a juvenile delinquent? She knew it, they were already mounting a whisper campaign. That *she* was the cause of Wesley's bad behavior. That she neglected the boy. That he acted up to get attention. Or that she pampered him, and he rammed into little old men to satisfy his spoiled whims. Hadn't Claire always looked down her nose at common folks? Or ... she slapped the countertop. The pain in her palm did not bother her, it only maddened her even more. The ringleader of the embargo was undoubtedly that Magda De Gryse. Everyone knew she was jealous of their successful life. Besides, Magda had an imaginary bone to pick with her, believing that Claire had murdered her cat Minous. The stupid animal had disappeared a few years earlier. Magda yapped all over town that Claire had poisoned the cat. Everyone knew the cat had just run off, and who could blame it, life must have been intolerable with that madwoman.

No wonder their daughters hardly ever came to visit. If anyone deserved the Nobel Peace Prize, it was Walter.

Claire slapped the countertop a second time. She refused to let it get under her skin. The customers would return once they'd had their fill of that foreign hormone-laced junk from the supermarket.

Herman and Wesley had been acting like a pair of unruly monkeys lately, but she would waste no time in reining them in. Her son's summons to juvenile court was a humiliation she must forget as quickly as possible. She peered out of the window. The sunlit street was abandoned.

She could permit herself a short break. She came out from behind the counter and went over to the glass-fronted refrigerator with aperitifs and wines. The 'boozerator', she and Herman called it. They used to stock canned vegetables and sauces, but that didn't catch on. They replaced them with wine and aperitifs, popular with novice alcoholics who wanted to write off their addiction as part of a Burgundian lifestyle. For what went better with a veal roast than a nice glass of wine? The seasoned alcoholics did not go to this amount of trouble. They unabashedly came to the butcher shop for their wine on days when the grocery was closed and, mustering up their last sliver of good manners, bought a dried sausage along with it.

Claire sniggered. She liked her daily glass of wine as much as the next person, but she kept it under control. She picked out a mid-range white, the best they sold. She opened the door marked 'PRIVATE', uncorked the bottle in the kitchen and drank her first glass in a single swig.

◆

Wes did not notice the pop of the cork, absorbed as he was in the reactions to his post on the social media site.

Eighteen friends had responded. The reactions varied from 'Whoa!' and 'Way to go Wes! ;-)' to 'Try just once to be a *hero*' and 'Wes makes a mess'. No reaction from her. Not yet. He quickly typed more details about what exactly had happened. Maybe she hadn't reacted because she wasn't sure if he was the good guy or the bad guy.

He scrolled to her name on his list of 'friends', opened her profile and clicked on her photo albums. Although 'Turkey-Antalya' and 'pool party' were certainly worthwhile, he selected the series 'Summer in Spain'. His heart pounded in his throat. Machteld holding a cocktail, Machteld with her parents at a Spanish market, Machteld at a Roman ruin. And then, Machteld in a bikini on the beach. He glanced up from the computer at the poster of Batman, and then at the clock on his nightstand. There was still time. He unzipped his trousers. He skipped the first pictures, even though these were the hottest poses. But there was some dopey Spaniard in the picture, which distracted him while jerking off. In the third picture, Machteld looked askance at the camera, smiling, hands on her hips, with a fine view of the curvature of her breasts. The picture also showed a snatch of her bikini bottom. Wes's dick hardened. He imagined how she would moan. He closed his eyes. Suddenly he saw the doorway of an employment agency, and in it a bleeding, homely girl in shabby clothes, and his erection withered.

◆

'Ms. Maes!'

Saskia hadn't gone but ten meters when hearing her name made her jump out of her skin. The short tug on his leash made Zeppos suspend his sniff along the wall. He returned to his owner, who looked over her shoulder at the two approaching police officers.

'Ms. Maes, could we have a word with you?' asked the first of them, once they had caught up with her. He put his hands on the small of his back as he caught his breath. Then he showed her his badge.

'Officers Hauspie and Huyghe from the local police.' Saskia looked from the red-faced one to the policewoman, who was young and attractive, about her own age, the type of girl who would have bullied Saskia at school because she smelled of farmyard and wore clothes ten years out of date. But Officer Huyghe smiled amiably, something she was not used to from young, successful women. All this friendliness made her blush, so she stared at the ground.

'Do you mind if we walk along with you?' the man asked. 'Your dog looks pretty keen to get some exercise.' He pointed to Zeppos, who barked back. Zeppos sniffed at Officer Huyghe, who crouched down to stroke his head. He was a smooth operator, her little charmer.

'What's he called?' Huyghe asked.

'Zeppos.'

'Nice name,' said Hauspie.

'Did you name him after Captain Zeppos?' Huyghe asked.

'You know, from the TV series?' Hauspie added.

Saskia recalled the name from her childhood, back when everything was still all right. She wasn't aware of its origins. Her mother often used to talk about a Zeppos. She just liked the sound of it. The perfect name for a sweet dog.

The woman petted Zeppos again and stood up. Saskia was not reassured by this friendly chat; on the contrary, it alarmed her. She knew what the police were here for. Granddad had been injured and it was her fault. And now she'd have to pay for it. The only thing to do was to keep quiet. Speech is silver, silence is golden, that's what Granddad always said, to which he usually added, laughing: and for women, speech is silly and silence is a full-blown gold mine. So she kept quiet. She turned and continued on her way. Zeppos trotted blithely ahead. Officer Hauspie came and strolled alongside her. Saskia tried to put on a brave face and walk with her head held high, but she'd much rather just crawl under a rock.

'Ms. Maes, we'd like to ask you a few questions about yesterday. Could you tell me where you were around twelve-thirty in the afternoon?'

'I was in the city.' She did not say it, she squeaked it. Zeppos discovered a lamp post, and tugged at his leash. If only she and Zeppos could disappear, just vanish into the masses and be left alone. Work, watch TV, shop for new clothes once in a while, or go to the carnival, like normal people.

'Where exactly in the city?'

'On the Nieuwstraat, reading job vacancies in the employment agency's window.'

Officer Hauspie nodded. 'There was an incident on the Nieuwstraat yesterday,' he said, 'around half past twelve.' He fell silent. So did Saskia. The policewoman walked behind them, probably silently mocking Saskia's clothes and her cheap shoes. Once they were back in the patrol car, she would probably nudge her colleague and make fun of her. They passed the lamp post before Zeppos had completed his inspection. She stopped. The officers stopped too. They were not going to let her go until she told them what they wanted to hear. She kept quiet until they resumed their questioning.

'Were you present at this incident?'

'I was reading the job advertisements at the employment agency. I wasn't doing anything wrong.'

'Ms. Maes, I only want to ask you a few questions as a witness. No one's accusing you of anything.'

Zeppos lost interest in the lamp post. Further up, at

those two boxwood shrubs in blue ceramic pots, it might be more exciting.

'Ms. Maes,' said the policewoman, 'your grandfather was involved in the incident. A boy on a bicycle rammed into him.'

Zeppos sniffed around the first buxus. He took a bite out of it.

'No, Zep,' Saskia said, and he obeyed.

'What a good dog,' Officer Hauspie said. 'He really listens to you. Quite a different story from my cat. She's ripped half my house to shreds, no matter how much I yell at her.' He smiled. Saskia did not smile back. That one word had only heightened her misgivings. Yelling, she didn't like that.

'According to the boy who ran into your grandfather, the man was assaulting someone,' Officer Huyghe said. 'A young woman. He allegedly hit her, shoved her into the doorway and then pulled her back out. Was that you?'

Saskia was startled. She blushed all the way to her teeth.

'Ms. Maes,' the attractive policewoman continued, 'your testimony is essential for our investigation. If you're the woman who was present at the incident, you're the only eyewitness. You could clear a lot of things up for us.'

Saskia no longer had a clear idea herself what happened yesterday. After the boy had pulled Granddad off her, she'd had a temporary blackout. How seriously injured was her grandfather? She had no idea. If she told them what she knew, it would only make things worse. Maybe she should never have left the farm. It was her home, she was safe there. She was incapable of standing on her own two feet. Everyone could see that. Right there, next to the buxus shrub with her dog, flanked by two police officers, unemployed, dependent on government assistance, the best thing that could happen was if the ground under her feet opened up and swallowed her forever.

'Granddad didn't assault me,' she said. The police officers fell silent, as though to digest what they'd just heard.

'But you did meet your grandfather yesterday, didn't you?'

'Yes, we chatted. Then I left.'

'So what did you and your grandfather chat about?'

'Granddad asked how I was doing since I've been living on my own. My grandparents are very protective. They've always taken good care of me. I'm really grateful to them. I don't want to cause any trouble.'

'Saskia, telling the truth won't cause trouble. The only trouble comes from *not* telling the truth.'

She felt like crying. Whatever she did, it was always wrong. Tell the truth, Granddad gets into trouble, don't tell the truth, she gets into trouble. She chose trouble for herself.

Zeppos tugged at his leash. After that delicious pee he was anxious to move on. But Saskia was unable to go any further. She turned and walked back to her apartment.

The police officers followed her, of course.

'Saskia, you ...'

Trembling, she inserted the key into the lock. She ignored the officers' looks. She slammed the door behind her and burst into tears, leaning against the door, which sent a searing pain through her wounds.

Outside, Officer Hauspie cursed.

◆

'God damn it!' Hauspie banged his fist on the hood of the patrol car. He opened the door on the driver's side and got in, his head bright red from anger and the heat. Huyghe slid onto the passenger seat.

'There's no point,' she said. 'She won't point the finger at her grandfather.'

'I don't get it,' Hauspie sighed. 'Why in God's name would she stick up for a guy who ruined her life?'

Huyghe patted him on the shoulder. 'Don't try to understand.'

'We'll have to wait until we can talk to the social worker,' Hauspie snapped. 'What was her name again?'

Huyghe shuffled through her papers.

'Dorien Chielens.'

'And when's she back from vacation?'

'July 22.'

'Damn, then I'm on leave myself.'

Huyghe laughed. 'First time I've ever heard someone swear because he's on vacation, Roger.'

Hauspie chortled. 'I'll leave it to you then. Hopefully Dorien Chielens will be able to get that girl to talk to us. I believe the Bracke kid.'

'It was a pretty stupid way to go about playing the hero. Can't let him off the hook entirely.'

'Of course. But there's a big difference between rescuing a girl from her crazy grandfather and running over an old farmer just for fun.'

'Saskia Maes confirmed having spoken with her grandfather. I think the judge will be smart enough to put two and two together, especially if you count the charges social services plan to bring against Grandpa Maes.'

'We haven't seen the last of old Maes. He'll try to dig up Saskia's address so he can have another go at her.'

'He's a loose cannon,' Huyghe agreed. 'An old yokel who talks with his fists.'

'I'll confront him with young Bracke's testimony. And with the other charges. See how he reacts.'

Hauspie clicked on his seatbelt and started the engine. Then he turned it back off and undid his seatbelt. He winked at Huyghe, who looked at him questioningly.

'Just have to take care of one other small piece of business.' He pointed across the street. His old classmate Walter De Gryse rode by wearing a blue postal uniform. In Hauspie's detective brain, a few pieces of the puzzle fell into place. He was out of the car before Huyghe could say a word.

◆

'Walter!'

The mailman turned his head, and had difficulty recognizing the man with whom he had smoked his first cigarette, and got drunk for the first time. Thereafter followed many more of both: cigarettes and drinking sprees alike. After Magda got pregnant they lost track of each other. Walter had quit smoking years ago. Judging from Hauspie's hacking fit upon reaching him, he apparently hadn't kicked the habit yet.

'Hi, Roger! Still on the Bastos?'

'No, Camel Lights.'

Walter grinned. Women's cigarettes—in the old days they wouldn't have been caught dead smoking one. The men shook hands, and Walter winced.

'What's wrong?' Roger asked.

Walter showed him his hand, which was still red and itchy.

'Had a roll in stinging nettle,' he said, choosing not to mention his irritated ass. It felt good to talk, so that his backside could have some relief from the torture of the bike saddle.

'Who rolls around in stinging nettle on the job?' Roger asked.

'You don't want to hear about it,' Walter laughed. Roger laughed along with him, but at once turned serious.

'Walter, I think maybe I do want to hear about it.' He

stood a little bit closer. 'See, I heard this story today. From an irate father on a boat.'

Walter felt as though he had just stepped in a pile of dog shit.

'I think the father is mistaken, that he's exaggerating somewhat,' Roger said. 'He's made some rather, eh, explicit accusations about a man in a blue uniform on a bicycle.'

He eyed Walter from head to toe, and then back up. He raised his eyebrows and pressed his lips together.

'And I match the description.' Walter tried to sound flippant. But he achieved just the opposite: his voice cracked. Roger sighed.

'Look, I know how it goes. Something innocent happens, and a child's fantasy, or the parent's, goes into overdrive. Father calls the cops, relays the story and lays it on extra thick just to make sure they'll take it seriously. You follow me?'

Walter nodded. So the Egoist called the police after all.

'Am I up shit creek?'

Roger roared with laughter. Even the attractive policewoman who had joined them chuckled.

'Up shit creek, ha ha, Walter, you're still a real card. Tell me, what happened exactly?'

Walter sighed; his night on the toilet and the saga of the Egoist were bad enough, but now he had to relate it all to an old classmate, and with that woman listening in too. Roger Hauspie and his colleague took note of his story with amusement, and when Walter went quiet, with a blush of embarrassment, Roger looked pensive.

'You could get fined for relieving yourself in the open and for public indecency,' he said. 'I wouldn't worry about the crapping. But public indecency, now that's another story, especially if there's a child involved. The courts are awfully skittish about it, what with all the pedophilia scandals these days. It could go on your record.'

Walter groaned. Roger was on a roll.

'And it's not something that just disappears, you know, after five or ten years. There's a whole rigmarole to go through if you want it wiped off your record. You know how things go in this country. On top of it, you're a civil servant, your superiors will have to be informed. So there's a chance of extra penalties.'

Walter squeezed his handlebars in the hope that he would wake up from a bad dream. He did not wake up.

'Maybe it won't come to that,' Roger consoled him. 'All depends on how the court sees it. I believe you're innocent. I told that windbag he had to come down to the station if he wanted to file a complaint. I doubt he will. He might just as well be shoving off with that dinghy of his this afternoon.'

Roger slapped Walter on the shoulder.

'I'd advise you never to have a shit or a piss at the side of the road again, though. That's asking for trouble.'

He sauntered back to the patrol car and took his place in the driver's seat. He called back to Walter through the open window. No air conditioning, apparently, for the police.

'Don't sweat it, these things tend to blow over. After twenty years on the force I've got a knack for knowing when they'll press charges and when not. This time I think not.'

He turned on the engine and while his colleague fastened her seatbelt he waved.

'My regards to ...' He hesitated.

'Magda.'

'Right, Magda.' He gave the thumbs up and drove off.

Walter prayed that Roger's knack wouldn't let him down.

◆

Jan was too tired to read the newspaper. He thumbed through it, glancing at the headlines and stopping at the showbiz news and comics. He skimmed the TV guide. Nothing to write home about, summer-evening fare was mainly old films and reruns of mediocre comedy series. Smiling, he observed a buff-tailed bumblebee—*Bombus terrestris*—as it attacked the lavender. He yawned and closed his eyes. He was pleased: since installing himself on the chaise longue in the backyard he had only been annoyed by the turbine three times. He was learning to live with it, slowly but surely, like a house pet being trained.

He was just thinking that he felt like a nice refreshing cola when the telephone rang. Catherine's footsteps approached and the ringing of the telephone was replaced by her friendly: 'Hello, Catherine Lietaer here.' She came out back and sat down on a teak garden chair. She was wearing a white dress. Jan's gaze glided from her feet (in elegant heels) to her knees, over her breasts and to her face. All that was out of place in her stylish appearance was the bulky cordless phone.

'Yes,' she said.

'I don't, but my husband does,' she said. 'Why do you ask?'

Jan hated listening in on half a telephone conversation.

'Oh, we hadn't thought of that. Well yes, my husband did, but not me.'

'The whole night might be exaggerating it a bit, but certainly ...'

'No, I don't know—' she rolled her eyes at him.

'May I ask what you—'

'No, I don't know if other people have become ill.'

She let her tongue hang out in exasperation and rolled her eyes again.

'No, you can't speak to my husband.' Jan gestured approvingly.

'He's not in bed. He isn't home.'

'No, you may not quote me. Good day to you too.'

She hung up.

'What was that all about?' Jan asked.

Catherine stared at the telephone, as though she didn't quite believe what she had just heard.

'It was a journalist,' she said. 'Wanted to know if we had diarrhea.'

Jan chuckled. 'Summertime journalism. They'll throw any old rubbish into the papers. Is this what they call news?'

'Apparently. He asked if we had eaten pâté. Herman's summer pâté.'

Jan scrunched up his brow. He stared at the turbine, then turned slowly.

'Herman's summer pâté?'

'You ate some yesterday. I didn't. And you're the only one of us with the runs.'

'D'you think it was the pâté?'

Catherine shrugged her shoulders. 'Could be. He asked if we knew anyone else who was suffering from this ... food poisoning.'

Jan whistled through his teeth.

'Food poisoning, now we're talking. Maybe the whole town spent the night on the toilet.'

'Or at least whoever has a taste for Herman's summer pâté.'

Jan grabbed the newspaper as though he could see the article already.

◆

Roger Hauspie took a bite of his sandwich, but with distaste. Ever since mentioning recently that he liked chicken salad, his wife put nothing but that on his sandwiches. By now he was sick of it. He chewed and swallowed mechanically, if only to allay his hunger.

'Roger, someone here for you.' His colleague from reception stuck his head around the corner. Roger did not respond, he just kept chewing and nodded at him to continue.

'He wants to lodge an indecency complaint. Shall I send him through?'

This can't be happening, Roger thought.

'Show him in,' he sighed. He wasn't sure how he felt—glad for a reprieve from the chicken salad sandwich, or sorry that the loudmouth had turned up after all. He was still pondering this when De Graaff came in.

Roger wadded up the aluminum foil and lobbed the rest of his lunch into the wastebasket. He stood up. 'Hello, Mr. De Graaff.'

'Good afternoon, officer. Here I am, to file that complaint.'

Roger nodded and offered De Graaff a chair.

'I've brought along a specimen, just to be sure,' De Graaff said, holding out a plastic freezer bag. In it was some brown crud, with bits of grass and buttercups stuck to the side. A piece of chicken climbed up Roger's esophagus. He gulped it back just in time.

'You needn't have done that, Mr. De Graaff. Well, give it to me and I'll take it down to the lab.'

He took the plastic bag and tried not to think about what was slushing back and forth in it as he walked to the men's room. He flushed the bag down the toilet, stood there for a moment to be sure it was gone and returned to his office. On his way he heaved three deep sighs.

'The lab will run some tests on your specimen, Mr. De Graaff.'

De Graaff stretched back, self-satisfied.

'Are you going to take my statement in regard to the

complaint? Open defecation and public indecency.'

'Certainly, Mr. De Graaff.' Roger opened the computer program for registering complaints. Then he leaned across his desk and looked the windbag straight in the eye.

'Before I take down your statement, I want to ask you if you're sure you want to go through with this. There will be an investigation no matter what. If we find the perpetrator, he'll have to appear in court.'

'I should hope so, yes.'

'But that doesn't guarantee a conviction. We believe the public indecency was unintentional. Do you follow me?'

'Why don't you explain.' De Graaff sat up straight, his hands resting on his knees.

'I'm afraid you don't have much of a case. The man was doing his business. You'll have noticed that the, eh, fecal matter was not exactly firm. The man apparently needed to relieve himself quite urgently, and you happened to witness it. The evidence points in the suspect's favor. If the man has a clean record, and there are no further reports of public indecency, chances are he'll be acquitted.'

'Acquitted? I doubt that.'

'In which case, moreover, he can then sue you for slander and defamation of character.'

'But that's insane! What's happened to the rights of an honest family man?'

'I'm not saying I don't believe you, Mr. De Graaff. I just want to advise you of the consequences should you choose to pursue this case publicly. Are you absolutely certain the man exposed himself to your daughter?'

De Graaff stood up and leaned over the desk, so close that Roger could smell the garlic on his breath.

'I am disgusted that you're shielding that filthy pedo, officer. If you don't take my complaint seriously and find that pervert quick, then I'll personally see to it that this hits the media, and big.'

'It's my duty to inform you of the possible consequences,' Roger said, and turned toward his computer monitor. 'Tell me exactly what happened.'

He positioned his fingers on the keyboard and began to type. Operation Whitewash had flopped.

◆

A blissful smile passed across Ivan Camerlynck's face as he leaned over the sink and peered at the upstairs neighbor's window. He was still chuckling about the telephone call he had just received. Magda De Gryse, despite having the runs, had not sat still today. Ivan told the journalist just enough to make the story plausible, but little enough to avoid libelous quotes making their way into the paper.

That fatso butcher had got what was coming to him. He was the kind of huckster who gave independent business-men a bad name: selling sausages and hamburgers under the counter, and grinding last week's garbage into pâté. And then flaunting his fancy cars and faraway jaunts in front of the rest of the town. It did him good to see the butcher's transgressions splashed across the newspaper.

Ivan needn't feel guilty. The authorities knew exactly what he sold and how much he earned. More than that: the state kept tabs on whether he sold enough cheap medicine. For the one businessman it was a Big Brother government, for the other, one that consistently looked the other way. It simply wasn't fair. And when the system is unfair, it is every citizen's moral duty to give justice a helping hand.

Ivan opened the telephone book. Surely someone else would be interested in Herman Bracke's pâté. He looked up the number and dialed it on the kitchen phone. While it rang, he leaned over the sink.

There was nothing to see in the window. All day long, no sign of beauty in the buff. Maybe tomorrow.

◆

Herman Bracke lay in bed, listened to the hum of the turbines and to Claire's snoring. He agonized. Every attempt to put his thoughts into order failed. His head was a squash court in which his thoughts bounced against the inside of his skull like the rubber ball against the walls. The juvenile court's social worker had sent Wesley home after he promised to see a psychologist. Herman pictured him eventually being sentenced to hundreds of hours of community service, which would only drag down his already pathetic grades, relegating him to jobs for losers and dropouts, while a thriving butcher shop was waiting for him. Or else the juvenile judge would turn him over to the adult court, which, to set an example, would sentence him to a full prison term, whereby he would fall in with the wrong crowd and turn into a revolving-door criminal.

It was his dream that his son would take over the butcher shop one day. Had he neglected him these past years? Had he spent too much time in the shop, allowing them to drift apart? No, Herman attributed Wesley's total lack of interest in the business to puberty.

Even his son's sudden vegetarianism did not worry him, furious as he still was about it. Deep down, Wesley loved meat as much as he did, Herman saw it in the way his eyes glistened whenever a sausage or lamb chop appeared on his plate. It had manifested itself back when Wes was a toddler and insisted on knowing how Papa made head cheese, and was only satisfied when, wearing an oversized apron and with his hands full of pork, he had produced a portion of his own. Carnophilia was in his genes, in his skin, in his bones, in his entire body. Wesley was a true Bracke! But with a criminal record he could forget a career as a small businessman. No self-respecting housewife would buy sausages from a jailbird.

The orange light that shone through the pinholes in the

metal shades moved up and down in time with his breathing. Up and down. In and out. He took a deep breath and closed his eyes.

Since the incident with the Blaashoek pâté he kept his insomnia from Claire. She did not understand how badly he suffered from fatigue, and he did not want to saddle her with more woes. Her solution always lay in the boozerator, a good reason not to bring it up. Moreover, he wanted to avoid provoking an argument.

This afternoon he had sneaked out to the doctor after bringing Wesley back from court. At the end of a lengthy conversation, during which the doctor had only nodded and mumbled as though Herman were at confession, he suggested earplugs or sleeping pills, both of which Herman refused. His attempt at earplugs earlier that week had failed miserably, and sleeping pills would be a slippery slope, a dead-end street of organized lethargy. It would be the end of him. The doctor had also given him a brochure for a sleep clinic. Herman knew the sleep clinic would not be able to cure his problem. At the clinic he would sleep like a baby. The problem was in Blaashoek, along the canal.

His own remedy still worked best. In the back room of the shop he had stashed a supply of energy drinks. Whenever he felt a wave of fatigue coming on, he would down one or two of those disgusting cans. This pepped him up temporarily. The only hitch was that the energy drinks made him a bit irritable. He was less able to tolerate noise. When the cleaning woman rattled her buckets, he chased her out of the shop. So what, if it was all a little less clean.

He knew full well he was kidding himself: the energy drinks were no long-term solution. But for the time being they did the trick. Until Wesley's court case was behind them this would be how he survived his insomnia and exhaustion.

5

Friday

There wasn't much that gave Claire enjoyment these days. One of her few little remaining pleasures, besides swigging white wine, was settling down with the newspaper in the morning with a cup of coffee and a piece of toast, while the sun dried the dewdrops and a little bird danced alongside the pond. What bliss, paging through yesterday's news while today's news gurgled from the radio. Wesley was still in bed, and Herman usually too, although his sleep-wake cycle seemed quite out of sync recently. The past few days she regularly woke up to him climbing out of bed in the middle of the night and grumbling as he trudged downstairs to watch TV or potter around in the butcher shop. If there was one thing men were incapable of doing, it was entering or leaving a bedroom quietly. Apparently it always had to be accompanied by stumbling, groaning, or another bodily noise, and, in the worst case, turning on all the lights and then leaving them on, as if they'd turn themselves off or someone else would do it. Which was always the case.

As always, Claire only skimmed the front page of the paper, for she was keen to read the comics inside. So she missed the small news item at the bottom of the front page. 'TOWN TAKES TO THE TOILET', it said, with a photo of the wind turbines along the Blaashoek Canal, and underneath, 'See p. 7'.

She poured herself a fresh cup of coffee while she chuckled at the comic strip. She admired the cartoonist's talent for thinking up a new joke every day. She took a bite of her bread, and the chocolate spread melted on her tongue. She smeared the chocolate paste much thicker than was good for her. She also saw to it that some stuck to the knife, which she licked off with relish. Sometimes, if she was sure no one saw her, she would dip the knife into the jar and lick the chocolate off it. And then she'd dip it back in, without rinsing it off first. Chocolate spread was addictive, and Claire was simply prone to addiction.

She drank her fourth cup of coffee, her next-to-last at breakfast. Often, mostly every other day, she would first drink half a bottle of fruit juice to quench her thirst. That wouldn't be necessary today, because yesterday, after the white wine, she had drunk a liter of water and taken a pre-emptory aspirin, and gone to bed early.

Her eyes floated over the headlines. At the bottom of page four she read a short article about African fortune seekers stranded on a tiny island near Italy. They had bobbed across the Mediterranean in a rickety boat. Poor devils, Claire thought. These were moments when you realized how good you had it. Actually she hadn't done so badly with Herman. If she kept a tight hold on the reins, if he did what she said, then he was a model husband. He worked hard and put in long hours. They made a decent living, although it could always be better. Herman's dreadful business sense all too often inspired him with harebrained schemes, such as renovating the garage into a café. She'd never heard anything quite so stupid. Where were they to put the Audi once the garage had been turned into a café? Of course Herman hadn't given that any thought. And what a ridiculous notion that tourists would flock to see the turbines along the canal. People couldn't care less about those turbines. No, Herman had about as much talent for business as she did for abstinence.

Herman devoted far more attention to the quality of his products than to turning a profit. His Blaashoek pâté was a success, but Claire didn't want to think about the hundreds of other creations he proudly displayed in the deli counter without a single customer asking for them. In a town like Blaashoek, average was good enough. Their customers had as little need for expensive and exotic *charcuterie* as they did for a three-star restaurant. Sausage with applesauce, that's what they wanted. And pâté for their bread. Claire knew what the market wanted, she felt it, she smelled it. She never passed up a commercial opportunity. That worthless sauce cooler had been Herman's idea, the successful wine cooler hers.

Lately, though, Herman appeared to be following her line of thinking. Or, better put, he resisted less. He made the simple meat products the customers wanted, he no longer argued with the supplier, he functioned on a kind of autopilot. In fact, this was fine. As long as he did not do any more stupid things like lie there snoring with his face in a container of pâté, and if he would pay more attention to his appearance (for his personal hygiene left a lot to be desired), then it was even more than fine. What did she have to complain about, compared to those poor wretches on that Italian beach?

Her wayward son, perhaps? His foolishness was a one-off affair. Nonetheless she would cut him no slack, he wouldn't set foot out of the house all summer. No more taking advantage of parental neglect. Wesley would not jeopardize their hard work any longer.

Herman's temper did worry her. In those rare moments that his eyes blazed, they burned brighter than ever. Then he would explode at her or Wesley, or chase the cleaning lady out of the shop when she'd hardly even mopped the floor. He would pace about, grumbling under his breath, like a science professor pondering a difficult equation, only suddenly to return to hacking into a rack of lamb.

She put her musings on hold. The radio was playing a song whose title she didn't know, nor the name of the singer, but that she enjoyed humming along with. She took a sip of coffee and turned the page of the newspaper. There, on page seven, was a large photo of Blaashoek.

She read the headline, reread it, and choked.

◆

'What a miserable article,' Jan Lietaer sighed. He could feel Catherine's breath on his neck. She read, wide-eyed, over his shoulder.

'Unbelievable,' she sighed. 'Poor Herman.'

Jan read the headline again. PÂTÉ BEHIND MASS DIAR-RHEA, it said. And with the kicker: TOWN TAKES TO THE TOILET. The article quoted several anonymous witnesses. Jan recognized them as Walter's wife Magda, and pharmacist Camerlynck. He wasn't surprised by the latter; the fellow had a mean streak. Camerlynck thought himself superior to the other shopkeepers in town. He never participated in year-end events organized by the business association, he was the only one who did not sponsor the local cycling race, he was the only one who did not buy pancakes from Bries, the local youth group. Bries numbered approximately five members, and their pancakes were inedible. But it's the thought that counts.

'And in front of the whole country, on page seven,' Catherine said.

He looked back at her, and just before he could savor her closeness, she pulled away slightly.

'Summertime, you know. *La morte-saison*. Nothing better

to print, and people lap it up.'

The article was an accumulation of half-truths and beefed-up quotes. Jan searched for a reference to the call Catherine had received, but there was no direct quote. It did say: 'Veterinarian Lietaer and Farmer Pouseele also took ill from Herman Bracke's Blaashoek Pâté, generally referred to by the residents of Blaashoek as "summer pâté".'

'I'm going to sue that sonofabitch journalist,' Jan said.

Catherine laughed. Jan thought he heard a trace of mockery, which hurt his feelings a bit.

'Why would you do that?'

'You told him not to quote you.'

Catherine bent forward again.

'He didn't quote me.' She patted him on the shoulder. 'But it's sweet of you to stick up for Herman.'

Jan grunted.

'It's not just that this article is mean-spirited, it could be curtains for the butcher shop.'

'Don't exaggerate, Jan. People are quick to forget.'

She patted him on the shoulder again and walked to the door.

'What do you say to a wok meal this afternoon?' she asked, her hand already on the doorknob.

'Or a barbecue tonight?' he asked.

'No, it's too hot for that.'

'OK, wok then.'

'Back in a bit,' she said. He watched as she left. He was contented, it felt like a kind of a rapprochement.

◆

Catherine forced herself not to look as she passed number 27. If she did, within ten minutes she would be lying in Bienvenue's bed. So she stared straight ahead. Still, out of the corner of her eye she noticed that the curtains were closed. She smiled and enjoyed feeling the sun on her face.

It did her good to ride her bike again, even though she had underestimated the force of the wind. She should have pumped the tires up firmer. Hard to believe that they lived barely a hundred meters from the butcher shop, and she always went there by car. Her bicycle stood rusting in a corner of the garage. She resolved to cycle along the canal more often. And maybe it was also a good idea to use the bike for her visits to Bienvenue. She could leave it in the downstairs hallway, rather than park the car out of sight.

The lights were on at the Brackes'. It showed some gumption; the newspaper article was reason enough to close up shop for a while. She parked her bicycle in front of the window. The shop was empty. Herman could use all the support he could get, and Catherine was determined to do her bit.

◆

Jan scanned the showbiz news and the comic strips—Garfield was fantastic again—and folded up the paper. Poor Herman, he thought, as the brilliant sun tried to lure him out back for target practice. Love to, thought Jan, but he couldn't allow yet another day to be shot to hell. Once in a while a person had to buckle down and work.

He got up, straightened his back and picked up the pile of letters from the table next to the window. He put them back, checked to see if there was any new mail in the box, and as there wasn't, picked up the stack again. He thumbed through them and noticed the letters for number 27. They were both addressed to the African. NIAY BAJI BIENVENUE was printed in block letters on the first envelope. The return address was for a mobile telephone provider. On the second envelope, his name, shortened to Bienvenue, was written in a curving, feminine hand. Jan planned to bring them around to number 27 after he'd had his coffee.

Nothing finer than gazing out at the garden with one's morning coffee. As long as those horrible shadows ... No, don't. He removed a coffee pad from the box, took a deep whiff of the aroma and placed the pad in the machine, which gurgled as it heated the water.

While he waited he brought the letters in from the living room. He set the two for the African aside and first tore open the bills with his right index finger. The first was for their internet and digital television bundle: sixty-five euros. For that amount, Jan thought, you'd think the internet connection could be a little faster. Not to mention the TV blackouts. Then there was an invoice from the town council for garbage collection. Pffft. And the newspaper's marketing department came whining for money too. Was the subscription up for renewal already? He briefly considered cancelling it, with an angry letter that he was disgusted by the article pillorying his townsman. That it was disgraceful—that's the word he would use, disgraceful—and unworthy of journalistic ethics. But then it occurred to him that the morning paper was an indispensable part of his morning ritual, and laid the bill neatly atop the other two. The last envelope contained an invitation for an open day at the Peugeot garage in the city. Catherine had bought her 207cc there last year. Did they really think he was in the market for a new car so soon?

The coffee! He was so engrossed in the mail that he forgot his coffee. He tossed the invitation onto the breakfast table and took the cup from the machine. He took a cautious sip, then downed the coffee in three gulps, his gaze fixed on the shadows that glided across the grass. *Whoosh whoosh whoosh*. He sighed, put the cup in the sink, and picked up the letters for the African.

Only now did he recognize the envelope with the feminine handwriting. There was small stack of identical envelopes in his desk drawer. But what truly sent a shiver down his spine, now that he inspected the handwriting more carefully, was the letter B. The familiar curl at the beginning of the letter from countless birthday cards, New Year's greetings and baby congratulations. Yes, he was certain of it, the B of Bienvenue was Catherine's B. He swallowed. The cozy atmosphere in the kitchen evaporated. As though a cloud passed in front of the sun.

He had to keep his cool. As a volunteer for the town council, Catherine occasionally had contact with asylum seekers. Perhaps it was an invitation for some or other activity. Hadn't she mentioned a barbecue being organized one of these days? And wasn't there a benefit event scheduled on the program, whereby the town council hoped to integrate newcomers into the community?

Then why just his first name? Or was it his family name? With Africans you never knew which was which. But still, why did she only write 'Bienvenue'? It suggested a friendship. Or more than a friendship.

He smelled the envelope. A whiff of perfume. He held the envelope up to the sunlight. There was a letter inside, but something smaller too, an opaque rectangular form between the sheets of translucent paper. The size of a snapshot.

Jan suppressed the urge to tear open the letter. If its contents were innocent, then he could no longer re-deliver it. He had to open the envelope discreetly.

The kettle. He hadn't seen it since they got the coffee machine. As he opened the cupboard underneath the sink, he hoped that Catherine hadn't given it away. Maybe it was sitting on Bienvenue's stove.

But no, there it was. He filled the kettle with water and placed it on the ceramic stovetop. He had to read the letter before Catherine came home. If she caught him, there'd be hell to pay. How long did it take for water to boil? An eternity, apparently. He circled the cooking island and held the envelope up to the sunlight a few more times. He shook it, as though that would help.

The kettle started to gurgle softly. When had Catherine left? Ten minutes ago? Half an hour? He sniffed the envelope again. Yes, he recognized that perfume. Had she sprayed it on intentionally, or was it simply a scent that by now had just seeped into the envelopes? He held his hand half an inch from the side of the kettle. Tepid.

He went to the table and looked at the Peugeot invitation. Although it didn't interest him a damn, he read the address, the date, the time, and the slogan: 'Discover our new models!' The photo featured a proud garage owner against a background of flapping banners and the most popular Peugeot models. Two blonde women in short skirts leaned against the cars. They were meant to give the slogan an amusing double entendre. Attractive women, but not as stunning as Catherine.

Again he examined the handwriting on the envelope addressed to Bienvenue. Was he absolutely sure it was Catherine's? Plenty of women had curvy and curly handwriting. The letter could be from anyone. He studied the numbers. No, he recognized the 2 and the 7 too. Damn it all!

The bubbling of the water caught his attention. He hurried over to the stovetop and held the letter above the steam. After a minute he gave the lip of the envelope a slight tug, but the glue had not loosened yet. Jan counted off four minutes. He occasionally turned the letter, like a sausage over a campfire. Then he tried again. This time the lip lifted. Jan turned off the stove. With his heart in his mouth he laid the envelope on the kitchen table.

He did not need to read the letter. The first thing that slid out of the envelope was a photo of Catherine. She was wearing the green dress she'd had on a few days earlier. Only she had pulled down the top, teasingly showing her breasts to the camera.

◆

'Hello, Herman.'

The butcher shop was empty, quiet and cool, like a mausoleum. Herman lifted his face, but his bloodshot eyes did not see her. He just stood there, as though she were an apparition.

'I'm really sorry about that article, Herman. It's so unfair and mean.'

Herman sighed. He shrugged his shoulders.

'They're right,' he said.

'Who's right?' Catherine asked. She felt awkward.

'The newspapers. They're right that the pâté was spoiled. I should never have sold it.'

She didn't know what to say.

'It could happen to anyone. It doesn't mean they have to put it on page seven of the newspaper.'

'I'm sorry Jan got sick. Did it last for long?'

Now it was her turn to shrug her shoulders.

'Oh, Herman, you know ... a bit of vomiting, a bit of diarrhea, just like with any—' she stopped short.

'Food poisoning?' Herman said it for her.

Catherine blushed.

'I should never have sold that pâté. You spend years building up a reputation, and it's wiped out in a single day. Everything gone to the dogs.'

'People have a short memory. Within a week they'll all be on vacation, and something new will crop up for them to raise a stink about. It'll blow over, you'll see.'

Herman smiled like a man on death row. He was completely spent.

'I'm very particular about the quality of my meat, Catherine. I use only the best products, so this is a bitter pill to swallow. Especially since I know I should never have sold that pâté.'

'I think you're brave to keep the shop open,' she said.

'I think you're brave to come and shop here,' Herman replied.

'So give me two chicken breasts, before I change my mind,' Catherine said with a wink. Herman did not react. Catherine wondered when his nerves would snap.

'Two chicken breasts,' Herman muttered as he took them out of the cooler.

'Where's Claire, by the way?' Catherine asked. She realized too late that she may have struck a sensitive chord again.

'Gone to see the lawyer. She wants to register a complaint against the newspaper, and against whoever it was that tipped the story.'

'Good for her,' Catherine said. Herman wrapped up the chicken breasts and told her the price. He ended with a question mark in his voice, which used to mean he expected her to order something else. Now, though, it was as though he was surprised she would be willing to pay for his meat at all.

'That'll be it,' she said. Herman put the packet into a plastic bag; the crinkle of the bag made the awkward silence between them even more excruciating. Catherine paid, thanked him hastily and shut the door behind her. No one had come into the shop while she was there, nor did it appear as though anyone else would.

◆

Jan sat in the easy chair, with the photo on the coffee table. The letter, in which she disclosed, in broken French, how much she missed Bienvenue, lay on top of it and just covered her breasts. Jan had always known. A woman like Catherine never stayed with a man like him forever. She was too refined and attractive to men with a more impressive career or physical appearance than his.

He had always known, and still he was surprised. More than that: he was shocked. Not by the fact that she cheated on him. That was bound to happen; he'd feared this from the moment he placed the ring on her finger. What made his stomach constrict like an empty potato-chip bag was the person she'd cheated on him with. He had always expected her to leave him for a surgeon, an Olympic athlete or a politician with a parliamentary mandate. But an asylum seeker, a man with the name of a doormat?

When he imagined how that man touched her, how he kissed her, how he peeled that green dress off her body, he wanted to gag, as though he'd just wolfed down a whole container of Blaashoek pâté. All the smutty fantasies that forced themselves onto him had taken place in an apartment not even a hundred meters from his own front door. Well, what's done is done, as the saying goes. He had to think ahead, of the future, of his life after Catherine.

Those were worries for later. Now that he heard Catherine's key in the front door, he stiffened. He braced himself for what was about to happen.

◆

She saw at once that something was up. He sat in the easy chair like a terminally ill patient, tense, his arms folded. He looked from her to the coffee table, and when she saw what was lying on it she knew that her life with him was over.

'You don't have to explain,' he said.

'Jan, I ...' He raised his hand.

'You don't have to explain. I just want you to pack your things and leave.'

'Can't we talk it out?' She went over to the sitting area and sat down across from him. She tried to do so elegantly, despite her trembling legs. She set the bag with the chicken breasts down next to her.

'There's nothing to discuss, Catherine. What could you possibly say? That you're sorry? That you didn't mean to hurt me? What's the point? Of course I'm hurt, of course you're not sorry. Or maybe you're ashamed of being clumsy enough to let me find out.'

'Jan, I ...'

'I figured you'd leave me sooner or later. Even though it's later than expected, in the end it's always a surprise. A real slap in the face.'

'Then let me explain. Please.'

'What's to explain? What do I care how you met, how long you two have been carrying on, what in him attracted you? He's black and broke, so I can well imagine what you fell for.' He laughed contemptuously.

'It wasn't about the sex,' she said. Not *only* about the sex, she should have said, if she were being honest. He dismissed her with a flick of his hand.

'I said I'm not interested. My mother was right, you know, you're no match for me.'

'Your mother,' Catherine sighed, and threw her arms in the air. 'If you'd listen to your mother a little less—'

'No!' he screamed. 'I should have listened to her *more*! If I had, I wouldn't be sitting here across from an adulteress!' The veins swelled in his neck. Catherine did not want to get dragged into a did-so-did-not argument.

'So what do you want?'

His eyes blazed.

'I want you to leave. Today. I can't stand the sight of you

anymore.' He picked up the letter and the photo and threw them in her face. 'And take these with you.'

'If that's what you want.'

'Yes, that's what I want. And don't worry, you'll get your share of my money.'

'I don't want your damn money.' She got up.

When she closed the door behind her to go upstairs and pack her things, she could hear him muttering from the living room.

'Parasite! Filthy whore!'

Her clomping around upstairs irritated him, the muffled sobs irritated him, the fact that she gave in so quickly irritated him. He wanted a fight, he wanted to curse her out, he wanted to hear her beg and plead and cry, here in the living room. After which he would not forgive her, but show her the door. Their discussion hadn't lasted even two minutes, and now she was packing her bags to move in with that Negro. As though she were glad, as though she looked forward to it. She was dying to get away from him so she could let that wild beast ride her. She had staged that whole charade with the photo, because she didn't dare tell him to his face. She wanted him to catch her and throw her out of the house so that *he* would be the bad guy and she could plunder his bank account. Not interested in his money, was she? He didn't believe a word of it. He sighed. He dared not tell his mother. He had an intense craving for beer.

Then the living-room door opened. Her eyes were red and swollen. She had changed into old, unstylish clothes.

'You're a sight for sore eyes,' Jan snapped.

'Everything you paid for, I'll leave here.' She stood there like an unresisting victim. And with a wry smile, she added: 'And I'll go by bike.' The door shut behind her.

'Ungrateful slut!' Jan gnashed his teeth and clenched his fists.

◆

Herman wiped down the counter for the third time. Since Catherine Lietaer—not only a beautiful woman but one with a heart of gold—had left, the bell on the shop door had not tinkled even once. He looked forward to Claire's return, so he could go back to the atelier and give the cold storage a good scrub. Everything had to go. Not only the two containers of spoiled pâté, but all the meat as well.

Tabula rasa. A clean slate. Claire would curse him, call him a wastrel, accuse him of not appreciating the value of money. She had blathered non-stop that he was obsessed with the quality of the meat, while the whole point was to make a decent profit. As a shop owner you couldn't rely on support from the state. And while this was all true, Herman could only regain the trust of his customers if he obsessed even more about quality.

He realized this was his last chance. He did not believe what Catherine said, that people forgive and forget. People forget the bad things about themselves, but when it's someone else, they forget only the good. Mistakes come back to haunt you, even years later. He could therefore only re-establish his reputation by working even harder, making even better pâté, serving the customers even better.

Herman took a can of Red Bull from the under the counter. His fifth today. A few hours ago he was at the end of his tether. Suicide seemed the only solution. Now, five Red Bulls later, he could face life again. He felt energized. He would not let them get him down, Herman Bracke was not one to throw in the towel without a fight. If they wanted to fuck with somebody, then not with him! Not anymore!

Perhaps it was better not to wait for Claire to get home before starting the big clean-up. Just let her find out after the fact. First he would clean the walk-in refrigerator, then mop the floor and the scrub the atelier—he had chased away the cleaning woman too often these past few days—and finally, make up a new batch of his delicious pâté. And he'd change the name too: from today onward it would be called Bracke's New Blaashoek Pâté. Or no, Bracke's Summer Pâté. Or better yet: Herman's Windmill Pâté! Those damned turbines would no longer ruin his state of mind, on the contrary, they would become his trademark. Herman's Windmill Pâté, a fine name for a new start! Herman chuckled.

He was just about to turn to the door of the atelier when the bell tinkled. It was not old Mrs. Deknudt, as he expected. It was a man he guessed to be in his mid-forties. There were large sweat patches under the armpits of his brown shirt. The shirt was tucked into a pair of gray trousers. The man's dull eyes were set in a sagging face and his expression betrayed an obvious desire to be anywhere but here.

Herman did not know the man. This worried him.

'Afternoon, sir,' he said.

'Good afternoon,' the man replied, in a way that suggested he had to say this often, and did not enjoy doing so. A salesman, Herman thought.

'Are you Herman Bracke, owner of Herman's Quality Meats?'

'Indeed I am,' said Herman.

'My name is Freddy Ghekiere. I am an inspector for the federal Food Safety Board.'

Herman nodded. Meanwhile he thought of the spoiled pâté in the walk-in refrigerator. His hands trembled. His shoulder blades itched and a sudden, sharp pain burned behind his eyes. He heard a hum, like from an idling car.

'I received a telephone call yesterday with a complaint about one of your foodstuffs.'

Herman thought of the atelier floor, which was badly in need of a scrubbing. The pain annexed his head and numbed his thoughts. He squeezed his eyes shut and reached for the chopping block. The hum now sounded like an idling truck.

'And this was in today's paper.' He held up the morning newspaper and Herman squinted at the picture of Blaashoek, with the wind turbines sticking out above the rooftops. The monsters.

'I think an inspection is in order, don't you?'

Herman grunted. The itch in his shoulders fanned out over his chest and made his heart race like mad. He clenched his fists.

'Can I first see your workroom?'

Workroom, he couldn't bear to hear his atelier be called that. Ten idling trucks resounded in his head.

'Did you hear me, Mr. Bracke? Might I see your workr—'

'No!!'

Herman screamed as the meat cleaver cut through the air. In those fateful seconds he wished he could grab it back and undo everything. But he could only look on helplessly as the cleaver sliced into Freddy Ghekiere's skull. It made no more noise than when he chopped into a cutlet. Blood and brains spattered onto the floor. Freddy Ghekiere crumpled and collapsed against the deli counter, where all that was left of his last breath was the condensation on the glass.

◆

Wes was startled by a yell. He closed the browser window, stuck his dick back into his pants and zipped up his fly. The scream came just ten minutes after the bell to the butcher shop had rung for the third time.

This morning there had already been a whopper of a ruckus. It was his mother's doing, as it often was. Only this morning it was worse than usual. Shouting and screaming, but to his surprise, not because of something his father had done wrong. This time someone else had screwed up. Shortly after her tantrum she left for the city: to the lawyer, according to his father. For a divorce?, Wes asked. His father did not laugh.

Was Ma back from the lawyer? Had she come back and opened fire already? Wes hoped Machteld would not prove to be such a difficult wife. Well, it was also a matter of cultivation, of course: his father pretty much invited it, with his spine like rice pudding.

Wes held his breath. He didn't hear a thing. If it were Ma, then he'd already have heard the living-room door slam, and after that the kitchen door, followed by the pop of a cork.

A new, drawn-out howl, like a lamentation. Every hair on Wes's body stood on end. Man, now he was really scared. Wes looked at the poster above the computer. Batman had seen his parents murdered when he was a child. Wes could read the reproach in those dark eyes: YOUR FATHER MIGHT BE LYING DOWN THERE FIGHTING FOR HIS LIFE, AND YOU SIT HERE SULKING IN YOUR ROOM, YOU PATHETIC JERK-OFF.

Wes cleared his throat and swallowed. He got up and cursed himself for his jelly-legs. He cursed himself again, because in order to jerk off in peace, he had locked the door. With his tongue between his teeth he turned the key. The door opened with a shrill squeak. If there was a murderer in the house, then he'd have heard it for sure.

In the hallway the parquet floor creaked like never before. He tiptoed to the stairs and leaned over the banister.

Nothing. He ignored the voice in his head which said that at this rate it would take him a year to get downstairs.

Wes pricked up his ears. He heard a soft pounding. It took several seconds for him to realize it was his own heartbeat. He stepped onto the first tread. It creaked. Wes took three steps at once. From the landing where the stairway made a u-turn, he peered down the ground-floor hallway. Still nothing. No murderer. No father. He went the rest of the way down the stairs. He heard a muffled sound.

He crept down the hall and opened the door to the butcher shop more quietly than ever. Sweat prickled his eyes. He wiped it off: a drop of salt in his eye could be fatal.

'Pa?'

He took another step.

There was blood everywhere. Blood on the counter. Blood on the wall. Blood on the boozerator. And there, in the middle of it all: his father, in a blood-drenched apron, leaning over a man with a cleaver in his head, wailing. Something gray oozed over the man's face.

'Pa?'

His father looked up. Blood on his cheeks, blood in his hair. His head twitched, his eyes bulged.

'Help me! For God's sake, help me!'

◆

Roger Hauspie popped the last bite of his Milano bread roll in his mouth as if it were the tastiest morsel he'd ever eaten. In the wastebasket the wad of aluminum foil with the remains of the chicken salad sandwich glistened like crime-scene evidence trying to attract his attention.

He swallowed the last bite and took a swig from a can of cola. Was the chief here yet? Yes, through the glass pane in the door he saw light reflect off his bald head. He took a deep breath, snatched the newspaper from the desk and went into the chief's office. Last chance for Operation Whitewash. He knocked and the chief looked up, distracted, from his computer screen.

'Ah, Roger. What can I do for you?'

'Frank, I've got a rather sensitive case on my hands,' he said. The chief raised his palms in the air.

'Two hours from now I'm going on vacation, Roger. Don't you dare come saddling me with tricky cases.' He laughed, but it was bad news all the same. Poor timing with the chief almost always meant: forget it. Still, Roger laid the newspaper on the desk. The chief read the page and frowned. Roger stared at the bushy eyebrows which, because of the smooth skull, commanded a more prominent place on his face.

'Blaashoek got hit by a bout of food poisoning yesterday,' Roger said. 'Pretty much everyone's got diarrhea.'

The chief looked amused. A smirk played across his lips. Roger saw his chances get a boost.

'The mailman too, Walter De Gryse. He had a bad case of the runs but went to work anyway.'

'Well, well,' said the chief. 'Now that's a rare thing these days, a civil servant with a work ethic.' He winked.

'He might have been better off staying home. It's like this ...' Roger slid a chair closer and sat down. The chief looked as though he considered it a breach of protocol. Then he leaned over as a sign that Roger should continue.

'On his way to Blaashoek Walter got an attack of diarrhea. He couldn't hold it in any longer and did his business alongside the canal.'

'Alongside the canal?'

'On the bank. Near the boat docks.'

The eyebrows scrunched together, like hairy snails preparing to mate.

'Ah, there. Not really the ideal spot to take a dump, I'd say.'

'Well, no, indeed. Yesterday a man filed a public indecency complaint. He claims that his daughter witnessed Walter De Gryse's, um, exertion. Says that the mailman deliberately exposed his genitals to the child.'

The chief sighed. 'How old's the kid?'

'Six.'

He sighed again.

'Do you know this mailman personally?'

Roger felt himself blush. He nodded.

'I want you to turn the case over to the Family Assistance Team,' the chief said. 'This is their department.'

'Yes, but ...'

'Roger, that mailman took a crap along the side of the canal. And on top of it he flashed his gizmo at that little girl.'

'He didn't fl—'

'Intentionally or not, that girl saw his shlong. Right?'

'Says the father.'

'You're personally involved, Roger. You know the man. You've got to turn it over to Family Assistance. They'll interview the kid. And the district attorney will take it from there. Period. You have to be careful with cases like this. Can't go sweeping all the crimes committed by people we know under the carpet, can we? Our colleagues will look into it, and if your mailman is innocent, then the judge will acquit him.'

The chief handed back the newspaper article. From the corridor came the sound of hurried footsteps. Officer Huyghe, red-faced, appeared in the doorway.

'There's been a murder,' she panted.

The chief bolted upright. 'Where?'

'In Blaashoek,' she said. She looked at Roger, who felt the blood drain from his face. 'At Bracke's butcher shop.'

◆

Rumors of what Wesley Bracke and the policemen had seen in Herman's butcher shop spread like wildfire. Although only four people—Herman, Wesley and the two forensic technicians who photographed and videoed the crime scene—had witnessed the remains of the bloodbath, the broadsheets confidently reported that Freddy Ghekiere had been found hanging from a meat hook and had been ravaged by an axe. According to the tabloids, he had been skinned and gutted like a sheep in an abattoir. The television reporters described how Herman had neatly chopped Freddy into pieces, as one might expect from a professional butcher. The spiciest particulars were to be found via the gossip circuit in town and on a wide range of internet forums, which provided graphic details of how Herman skewered the poor inspector alive, dispossessed him of his intestines, and then proceeded to chop off first the arms and then the legs. Herman was planning, according to 'well-informed sources', to cover his tracks by processing the inspector's flesh into pâté and setting the victim's car on fire off in the woods. Where all these well-informed sources got their stories remained a mystery.

Nevertheless, all the public prosecutor would say was that the victim had been 'grievously assaulted'. So the general public, unsated by such dry commentary, took matters into its own hands.

Freddy Ghekiere's murder had certain consequences for the other residents of Blaashoek as well. For starters, son Wesley saw his collision with old Maes splashed all over the media, as a possible basis for father Bracke's sudden display of brutal rage. Which precisely was the cause and which the result—the violence of the son or that of the father—would provide psychologists with discussion material for years to come.

For Walter De Gryse, the murder meant that his public

indecency case slipped out of the limelight. When someone has been murdered with a meat cleaver, nobody's interested in a loose willie. This is self-evident. The Family Assistance Team of the local police did not abandon the dossier altogether, but by the end of the weekend it was old news.

And as so often happens, the gravest consequences were reserved for those who actually had nothing at all to do with it. Some people are simply born unlucky. Saskia Maes was one such person. Others dig a pit for someone else, and fall into it themselves. Magda De Gryse was one such person. The weatherman had predicted storms for Sunday. But it looked as if the tempest was ready to hit Blaashoek on Saturday.

Saturday

Saskia Maes woke up to wetness and smacking. She opened her right eye and saw thick whiskers and a wet snout. The snout came closer and started lapping her lips. She pushed the face away.

'Ugh, Zeppos, don't!'

The dog yipped cheerfully, placed its front paws on her chest and licked her again. She let him.

'Yes, yes, I love you too.'

She slid out of bed, for there was no other way to temper Zeppos's enthusiasm. She rubbed the sleep from her eyes and in doing so tried to rub out the awful thoughts that had plagued her all night. Around 3 a.m. she awoke from a dream where she was on trial for murdering her grandfather. The courtroom was packed with young policewomen, and the judge was a cranky old farmer she had known as a child. Zeppos defended her, without success, because no one could make any sense of his barking. Only Saskia understood him, and she thought his defense thorough and moving. The judge and the public, however, ridiculed him. Without much fuss—as old farmers are wont—the judge sentenced her to death. Just as the blade of the guillotine was about to slice through her vertebrae, she bolted awake.

She put on her slippers and listened. Zeppos pricked up his ears. There had been talking and scuffing in Bienvenue's apartment all night. After her nightmare she drifted in and out of sleep, partly thanks to the pain that would long remind her of the confrontation with Granddad, and for a while she lay listening to the goings-on upstairs. It was not over yet, from the sound of it. Now she heard quiet sniffling. It couldn't possibly be Bienvenue. If anything, the big, buoyant man would cry out loud.

It wasn't her business. It did not surprise her that Bienvenue had a visitor, he was a good-looking man. Nor did it surprise her that the woman was crying. Bienvenue was no doubt a heartbreaker. She smiled and padded to the kitchen to make coffee.

'Come, Zep, time for your crunchies.'

The kitchen was bathed in sunlight. Not a drop of rain had fallen all week, and only at night did the temperature drop below 25°C. She yawned. She expected it to be a lazy day. Despite the heat she looked forward to staying indoors. Indoors she was safe, indoors her wounds could heal. Confrontation lurked outdoors. She opened the cupboard under the sink and took out Zeppos's dry food. She poured some into his bowl, and while he gobbled it up she opened the fridge to prepare her own breakfast. She was startled by the emptiness that stared back at her.

Amid the clamor and cursing upstairs, Saskia sat down at the kitchen table to butter her bread. Zeppos jumped up against her knees. She nudged him back.

'Calm down, little guy.'

How could she expect that bundle of energy to stay calm? There was no getting around it: groceries or no, Zeppos still needed to be taken out for his walk.

◆

Pain, pain, pain.

Jan Lietaer groaned. God, the pain!

He muffled a moan in the pillow. What time was it? He groped for the nightstand. Quarter past nine. He grumbled, hawked up a wad of phlegm, swallowed it and buried his head back in the pillow. A dinosaur was dancing on his brain. He hadn't felt so miserable since ... He had to stop and think. No luck. Since very long ago.

He opened one eye and looked off to the side, into the void. He and Catherine had slept in separate rooms for some time, but now the emptiness felt different, irrevocable, definitive. Until yesterday evening there was a chance, no matter how small, that she might come and lie down beside him once again. That they would make love in this bed, lie in each other's arms. He would snuggle up to her and feel her warmth. This is what he subconsciously lay waiting for, all those nights he spent tossing and turning, and all those mornings he woke up here, alone. He was waiting for the moment that he would open his eyes and she would be lying there, that she would smile at him, that she would hold him. Every day that she lived here, this was possible. And only now did he truly realize that it was a pipe dream, that such a scenario existed only in his imagination.

He sighed deeply. He let out a loud fart. No one heard it. He had to get up; this was going to be a trying day. Tell Mother the news, call the lawyer, deal with the administration, in short: prepare to do battle with Catherine. Even though she had left by bike, she was sure to come back for the car. And the rest.

He swung his feet out of bed. *Ninety-nine bottles of beer on the wall*, he hummed as he slid his feet into his slippers, *ninety-nine bottles of beer ...* His bathrobe felt like an abrasive sponge. He opened the door and heard nothing.

A total void washed over him. Just one less person and it felt like life itself had been wiped clean. This was no longer the house he had lived in. This was another house. Even though the mercury had risen to 30°C outside, he shivered. The stairs creaked louder than usual. And then he realized what really was missing. The smell of coffee. The two cups of coffee Catherine drank if she got up before him. The smell of coziness. The smell of a pungently sour pie in the sky, he knew now.

Now. He mustn't think of that word. Now was not something to look forward to, while she ... Yes, what was she doing now? Spreading her legs. Was she rubbing his afro between her breasts right now? Massaging his back? Sucking his dong? Jan pounded his fist against the wall.

He went downstairs and opened the living-room door. The sunlight insulted him. His mood was more suited to an autumn day, not one where jolly families built sand castles on the beach or sailed toy boats on a pond. Little birds frolicking in a bird bath, bees buzzing happily from flower to flower—it all made him want to puke. Ah, puking: his first good idea today.

That could wait till later. First drink some water, and take an aspirin. He chugged down a glass. The water tasted like rancid cheese biscuits. Nevertheless he filled another, which he downed as easily as the first. He drank a third glass, this time not forgetting to swallow the aspirin along with it.

Jan belched. He looked out into the yard, cursed the turbine and decided that cheerful, cozy mornings should be banned from now on. He ignored the urge to get the weekend paper from the mailbox and curl up with it on the sofa. He shuffled to his workroom.

All right, what needed doing today? He'd skip the puking, on second thought. He had to tackle all kinds of practicalities before his mother had the chance to berate him, so that he could prove he was a go-getter and not a doormat. He wanted to have everything sorted out before his mother could butt in on his misery.

He took a sheet of paper from the printer. He dug around in the desk drawer until he eventually found a felt-tipped pen.

Jan hesitated for a moment, and then wrote:

SEEKING:

PART-TIME SECRETARY M/F

Part-time, he couldn't afford more than that. His mother would be satisfied that he was at least pretending to maintain his income. Still, he mustn't have any illusions, she always found something to lambast him for. *Part-time*, he could hear her sneer, not enough work for a full-timer? No, he did not have enough work for a full-timer, she knew that full well. And now that Catherine was about to raid his bank account, frugality was the name of the game.

◆

An hour before Jan Lietaer hung the job vacancy notice in the window, Magda De Gryse sat on the sofa, newspaper on her lap, as though hypnotized. A single thought resonated in her head: *it's not my fault.* She looked at the photo of the chubby, smiling butcher and the smaller photo of the murdered health inspector. It's not my fault, Magda told herself. Herman was responsible for the hygiene in his shop. Herman had sold spoiled pâté. These facts were continually interrupted by the awareness that while she might not be to blame for Herman's crime, she did carry some responsibility for the consequences of her own actions. If she hadn't called that journalist, the town's night-time bout of diarrhea would be nothing but a bad memory in a week or so. But now it had more or less triggered a murder.

She took a tissue and blew her nose, while tears prickled her eyes. For the third time she read the front-page teaser. Then she opened the paper and reread the boxed piece about Wesley's aggression against an elderly man. There was obviously something not right with that family. Something Magda knew nothing about. Ergo, something she could not be held accountable for. Besides, a negative newspaper article didn't give you carte blanche to go and kill someone. Really, you don't impale a man on a meat hook and chop him into beefsteaks just because you took a knock in the press? There was something so wrong with Herman and his ostensibly happy little family that no one except them could be held responsible for that horrific scenario. Certainly not Magda.

The phone rang. She looked at it as though she could telepathically silence it. It kept on ringing. Maybe it was one of their daughters. Or it could be another journalist, which is why she did not answer. Walter came into the room.

'Aren't you going to answer it?' He walked over to the telephone table.

'I don't want to talk to any journalists.'

'It might be Lisa or Laura.'

She shook her head and brought the tissue to her right eye.

He stood in front of her.

'It's not your fault.'

The telephone went silent.

◆

Saskia took a deep breath, braced herself and opened the door. Zeppos charged into the heat of the day and in doing so dispelled Saskia's indecisiveness. She blinked in the bright sunlight, and after two tugs on his leash Zeppos understood that she wanted to go left instead of right. As soon as he caught on, he dragged her behind him like an aimless but determined leader, without a clue where he was headed. Saskia kept her eyes glued to the sidewalk, she studied the moss that grew between the paving stones and counted them. Another twenty and she'd be at the butcher, she knew by heart. She sensed some commotion at the butcher shop, but didn't dare look up. She used to do the same at school, when she suspected a group of classmates was cliqued together further up. All she wanted was to go in, buy some meat, walk to the other end of town with Zeppos so that he'd have had his daily exercise, and go home.

She focused on the cracks in the sidewalk. There were lots of them. They were old paving stones, maybe even from before the war.

'Ma'am, what do you make of yesterday's dramatic events?'

She did not want to look at the owner of the voice, but had no choice, thanks to a light that shone directly in her face, like a police floodlight. The light came from a camera perched on the shoulder of a man at the questioner's side. She was an attractive, smartly dressed woman with an expression that hovered between authority and arrogance, and she blocked Saskia's way as she repeated the question. The butcher shop, she now saw, was roped off with police cordons.

The young woman shoved the microphone under Saskia's nose, defying her not to answer. When she remained silent, the woman moved on to a new question. She held the microphone like a bludgeon.

'Had you ever suspected your butcher might be a murderer?'

Saskia gaped at her, astonished.

'You haven't heard?'

Saskia shook her head.

'Your butcher murdered a food safety inspector. What do you think of that?'

'That's terrible,' Saskia whispered. Suddenly she was much less aware of the journalists. Herman the butcher? That nice man with the friendly wife? How could he murder anyone?

'Did you notice anything strange lately? People say the hygiene in the butcher shop left a lot to be desired.'

'I ... didn't notice anything.' A flush rose to her cheeks, as though she'd sat in a steam bath for too long. I'm the only one who didn't see it, she thought. The whole town saw it coming, except for me.

'Did you know the butcher well?'

'No,' Saskia squeaked. Zeppos tugged at his leash, he wanted to move on, just as she did. The interviewer pulled the microphone back, perhaps aware that she'd already gotten the best shot of Saskia, a shot that would dominate the afternoon news: Saskia's shocked expression when she heard that the friendly neighborhood butcher was a cold-blooded murderer. A new tug on the leash was the perfect excuse to end the interview.

'My dog's eager to get going,' Saskia whispered, but neither the reporter nor the cameraman could make out what she said, nor did they seem to be interested any longer. The woman pointed to a house across the street, the cameraman nodded, and they turned away.

All sorts of thoughts whizzed through Saskia's head. Was this one of those hidden-camera jokes? She glanced back again. The police cordon was still there, and the news crew was now pestering an elderly man, who tried in vain to shake them off. He raised his arms in a gesture of surrender and then told them what he knew.

So it was true: Herman had murdered someone. But why? Saskia remembered him as a mild-mannered, amiable man. Had she been too naive? Maybe that friendliness was only a ruse to sell more meat. Perhaps he gossiped about people behind their back, while moments before he had greeted them warmly with 'good day' or 'till next time'. Might he have murdered her too? If she'd been alone in the shop today … She shivered.

But now they'd arrested him; that was good news. She was starting to like it here in Blaashoek, and wanted to hold onto that feeling of living in a safe cocoon. Blaashoek had to become her new home, the place where she could be happy. Then the thought crossed her mind: now that they'd nabbed a murderer here, Blaashoek was safer than ever. There couldn't be *two* murderers in such a little town, could there, she giggled. Out of the question.

'No, heh, Zeppos, no chance of that,' she said, crouching down to cuddle the dog. He licked her hand. Her thoughts had distracted her, and by now they were already on the other side of town. Something sparkled, attracting her attention, and that sparkle led her gaze, like a pointing finger, to a window. In that window hung a sheet of paper. It was sloppily written, but what it said made her heart leap.

SEEKING:

PART-TIME SECRETARY M/F

◆

Roger Hauspie was peeved. He had sacrificed his free Saturday at the altar of labor ethos. Not willingly, mind you, because he was not one of the select group of officers assigned to interrogate the deranged butcher. He and Huyghe had to keep the place running while the others tried to unravel the Blaashoek killer's motives.

Roger sat in the dingy canteen, where normally he only noticed the hum of the vending machine. Now he sat peevishly watching commercials on the television that hung on the wall above the bulletin board. The TV was for watching soccer matches on slow evenings, or for following the news if 'something serious' had happened. The last time 'something serious' happened was last year, when it turned out a policeman from Ieper had killed five people. The country was up in arms. And heads rolled within the police force. Two days after he had been fired, the director of the judicial police dropped dead of a heart attack. The canteen was too small for all the policemen wanting to catch the afternoon news those days, and he recalled the jeering and cursing when the serial killer appeared on camera. Today there would be no jeering; Roger sat there all on his own. His irritation was not brought on by the idiotic commercials, but by the sheer number of them, and every commercial was one too many when you were waiting for the news.

He poked at the salad his wife had prepared for him out of sympathy for his having to work today. That's why I love her, he thought. For the small, kind things she did for him. No doubt he'll be getting salads now for the next year to take to work. He chuckled, but regained his composure when the last programming announcement—finally—finished and the news intro began. He shoved the salad to one side.

The murder was the top story. The presenter summarized the events of the previous day and promptly switched to an interview with a forensic psychiatrist, who blah-blahed about mental accountability and the distinct possibility that Herman was a serial killer. Roger sighed. There they go again: one murder and they start combing the cellar in search of the nation's missing girls. The psychiatrist, with his unruly hair, gruesomely droopy eyes and five o'clock shadow, looked like a psychopath himself. You have to be a psychopath to recognize one. Court psychiatrists, the quacks of the modern age.

The presenter, none the wiser, brought the interview to a close. They were good at that, psychiatrists: meandering around an issue until everyone was bonkers. The presenter was replaced on screen by a street Roger recognized. Just a bit further up, the day before yesterday, he had had that talk with Walter De Gryse. A female reporter came into view. She had been given the task of pestering the locals with questions they could not answer. The only people who could answer questions in this kind of situation were windbags.

The reporter said something that escaped his attention. Then the woman vanished like a chimera. A new face filled the screen. Wan, weary, more scarred by life than was good for her. It was a face that evoked only sorrow, because whatever beauty had been there had withered before it had the chance to blossom. A wave of sadness washed over him.

Saskia Maes looked into the camera like a child expecting to be smacked. The more she got the gist of the journalist's questions, the greater her stupefaction. She spoke so quietly that the studio's editors had subtitled her. Like the forensic psychiatrist, she had no answer for the reporter's asinine questions. No, she hadn't noticed anything. No, she hadn't expected this. Roger leaned back. Then the blue ribbon at the bottom of the screen caught his eye. In it he read the word 'Blaashoek', just as the camera panned from Saskia to the closed butcher shop. Roger looked at the soda machine for three seconds, bit his bottom lip, and thought: *shit*.

◆

I want your love love love love, I want your love!

Wes hummed along while eyeing the manager of the record store. He held onto the headphones and swayed his head with the music. The girl looked at him and smiled. She was wearing a crop top. A navel ring glittered from her midriff. Inviting breasts. She turned toward the rack of CDs. Nice ass. She turned and smiled again. Wes blushed.

'Good, isn't it,' she said.

Wes nodded. Did she know he was the son of a murderer, he wondered.

'Want to buy it?'

'Nah,' Wes said, too loudly. He took off the headphones and left the store. Music didn't really interest him. Sometimes he would download a song, he regularly swapped MP3s, he clicked on links to YouTube now and then, but he wasn't a fan of any group, and half the time he couldn't name the performer. He simply consumed it, which is what he did with most things.

He let his eyes get accustomed to the sun. It was hotter in the city than in Blaashoek—there, you at least had a bit of breeze. The wind didn't stand a chance amid the tall buildings, which turned the city into an oven.

He had roamed through the city all morning and wondered if the rest of his life would be like this. Continually checking to see if people recognized him, *the son of the Butcher of Blaashoek*. His life would never be the same again. Wes himself had not changed, but everything around him had. It all looked different from yesterday. Threatening, hostile, aloof. He hadn't received a single text message. As though he suddenly no longer existed. He no longer felt at home on these streets.

He hadn't slept much last night. As soon as he fell asleep, he bolted awake. If he closed his eyes, he saw his father with the meat cleaver. His father in a pool of that dead guy's blood. His father who suddenly looked up at him. Those eyes. He knew he had more sleepless nights ahead of him.

Wes hardly remembered anything from the police interrogation. His previous encounter with the police, when he had run over that old pervert, made much more of an impression on him. Maybe you only had enough energy for one big impression at a time, and yesterday nothing could beat that look in his father's eyes. Man, all of a sudden his own arrest for assault and battery and the talk with the juvenile court's social worker were so futile. He felt the tears well up, because he recalled how his father stuck up for him, how he—quite unlike his mother—did not tell him off, but only gave well-meant, concerned advice. He swallowed back the tears. The fact that people stared at him was bad enough, but to see him cry, that was too much.

Cry: that is what his mother had done the entire day, when she wasn't being questioned or exploding into hysterics. The police put them up in a safe house belonging to the town council. The butcher shop had been turned inside out, just to be sure, and to be honest he had no desire ever to spend another night in that house. He was indifferent to the dump they'd put them up in, he had switched off his feelings. The stench of cat piss, the mold on the walls, he didn't give a damn.

His mother cursed and caterwauled, her mood dancing back and forth between fury and despair, and she barreled through the hovel like a crazed circus elephant. In the evening, exhausted from her mood swings, she sent him to the supermarket up the road to buy her a few bottles of wine, and she entrenched herself, booty in hand, in the bedroom with the flowered wallpaper and the damp-stains. This morning he ignored her drunken squalling.

After a quick wash in the filthy bathroom and an attempt to force two spoonfuls of corn flakes down his throat, he went outside to amble through the city and try to clear his thoughts.

Without success. In the house he felt oppressed, and on the street he felt unwelcome. Back to his mother then. Her drunken stupor must have developed into a mean hangover by now. He would soon be on the receiving end of a cascade of rebuke and abuse, not only directed at him and his father, but at all of Blaashoek and, if at all possible, the entire world.

Although he knew he was only putting off the painful confrontation, he lingered just a tad longer in front of the lingerie shop. A gorgeous brunette on a poster shoved her bosom proudly forward. That bra would look great on Machteld. How he yearned to give her that bra as a present. Well, he could forget that now. He bit his lip and wandered further. At the employment agency he wondered what had become of the girl. Had she found a job? He sighed. Would he ever find a job? He ambled further, his hands in his pockets and head hanging.

His temporary abode was ideal for a blind person. You could hear the loud house music blaring from the neighbors' window a hundred meters away. A good dance number was one thing, but Wes hated this *gabber* stuff. He hated this street, the dreary bleakness. Whoever lived here was doomed.

He opened the door and was met by a sweet stench. The odor did not come from the walls or the carpeting, but from the figure that lay sprawled on the stairs.

It was his mother. The tread where her head rested was covered with puke. She did not move. He would have to go up the stairs to help her. He would have to straighten her out and lay her in bed, as his father used to do.

Wes did not. He shook off a cold shiver and sidled along the wall past the stairs. He was careful not to breathe. In the kitchen he sat down at the breakfast table. For a few minutes he looked at his hands and stared through the window at a wall whose white paint was peeling off.

Wes flipped open his mobile phone. Not a single text message. He dialed the emergency number and hesitated. She was no longer alive, she was dead. But he had been mistaken with that old guy too. The only way to be sure was to go back there and feel her neck. But he dared not budge. He kept staring at the wall, at the paint that peeled like dead skin. He shoved the phone away.

He held his breath and listened to hear if she made a sound, whether she choked out the last slosh of vomit, whether she scrabbled back upright and wobbled into the kitchen. He dearly hoped to hear this, that she had saved herself.

It remained silent, except for the dull thud of the neighbors' house music. A beat that, ironically enough, reminded him of a heartbeat. Years later he would lie awake with the idea that he had murdered his own mother that afternoon by sitting at a table in a dirty kitchen, while he could have saved her life by climbing half a flight of stairs.

Wes sat there for about an hour, looking and listening, waiting for a mother. Then he made the decision to leave. He ignored the staircase—and the mass that lay on it— and slammed the front door behind him. Again he dialed the emergency number on his cell phone. An operator answered. He told her the address and hung up. Then he looked for the nearest bus stop. He would return to Blaashoek one last time.

◆

Saskia Maes hesitated no longer. This was a chance in a million. A job within walking distance from home, at the vet who had treated Zeppos so kindly. A dream! And with a bit of luck, the dream would become reality for her this afternoon. She checked her appearance in the bathroom mirror. She put on her prettiest T-shirt and her best jeans. Should she wear mascara? She once bought a tube of it at the drugstore, but didn't dare put it on, she didn't know how.

'What do you think, Zep?'

Zep was unimpressed. He sauntered off to the kitchen. She followed him.

'You have to behave now, Zeppos honey. I'm off to apply for a job. Be glad you don't have to!' She cuddled him, he licked her ear. She let him into the courtyard and quickly closed the sliding door. Zeppos came up to the window and barked.

'Shh, Zeppos, I won't be long.' He barked again.

She felt strangely giddy, as though she had a date with a pop star. Before she closed the kitchen door she noticed Zeppos staring at the turbine, his ears pricked. Good, that should distract him. Her hands trembled as she pulled the front door shut. Her mouth was dry. The street was deathly quiet, the camera crew had left and the town had retreated into itself, as if to gather its thoughts.

◆

Ivan Camerlynck locked the door to the pharmacy. He had stayed open a half-hour longer than usual, until one o'clock, waiting for Mrs. Deknudt. She did not come by. What's more: no one at all had come by. Apparently the town had gotten over the runs.

He would stop by Mrs. Deknudt's in person then, and most of all looked forward to settling down to his lunch of sausage and mashed potatoes with applesauce. With the takeaway meal from the department store in the city, his weekend could begin. Then he would scour all the websites and TV broadcasts for news about the Butcher of Blaashoek. He chuckled. Who'd have thought that his telephone call to the food safety authorities would give rise to such a spectacle. Wonderful, wasn't it, how things always worked out. If it rained tomorrow, then the perfection would be complete, for by now he was sick to death of this heat.

While his meal rotated in the microwave oven, he peered up at the African's window. There was some movement, but he couldn't make out if the woman was there. One thing was for sure: the shabby downstairs girl was out, because the dog barked as though twenty cats were hanging on its tail.

Ivan sighed. You work hard all week, and then the jobless don't even grant you a peaceful weekend. He peered up again. Yes, he just saw a lock of hair. Or was he dreaming? The beep signaling that his meal was ready released him from his reverie.

He opened the microwave, took out the plastic container, tugged at the cellophane wrapping and cursed when only the pull-tab tore loose. He took a paring knife from the counter, had another quick glance upstairs, and sliced the plastic film from the container just as he imagined a surgeon sliced open a patient's stomach.

The mashed potatoes were dry, but otherwise delicious. The sausage was juicy, although he considered emailing the manufacturer that they might make the skin a bit less tough. He mashed the applesauce into the potatoes, to give them more body. What more could a single man require in a meal?

Some peace and quiet, that's what. Quiet that he was not granted. Was that dog still not used to that stupid turbine? Ivan put aside the half-eaten meal and went out into the courtyard. Like the last time, the dog focused on the turbine for a moment longer, only to start barking at the wall.

'Shut your trap,' Ivan hissed. The dog barked louder.

It was much too hot out to stand here arguing with a dog. What could he use to bash the creature's head in? Then he got a better idea.

◆

The elevator bell announced the third floor. Hauspie and Huyghe got out, walked past the nurses' station and knocked at room 312. Roger raised his eyebrows at his partner and opened the door. An old man lay sleeping in the bed next to the window. Only a faint snoring betrayed that he was still alive. The bed nearer to the door was empty.

Roger cursed. He knocked on the bathroom door.

'Mr. Maes?'

He knocked again and opened the door. No one.

'Damn.'

He went back into the corridor and hurried to the nurses' station. He drummed his fingers on the countertop until a nurse turned up. He guessed that she was pushing fifty, and thus had seen every category of difficult family member at her desk.

'How can I help you, sir?' She sat down on a swivel chair and turned toward a computer.

'We've come for Mr. Maes. Gerard Maes.'

She tapped at the computer keyboard.

'Mr. Maes, that's room 312.'

She looked from Roger to Huyghe as though trying to ascertain the familial relationship.

'He's not in his room,' Roger snapped.

'Oh?' The nurse came out from behind the desk and shuffled to the room. Roger and Huyghe followed.

'He's not there,' Roger said.

'Maybe he's on the toilet,' the nurse replied, and pushed open the door without knocking.

'Hallo, Mr. Delannoy,' she said, but the man in the far bed kept on snoring. She opened the bathroom door.

'He's not there,' Roger said.

'Strange,' the nurse said. 'He's not there.'

Her eyes went wide.

'When we went in to collect the lunch trays, he was lying there watching the news. Maybe he went down to the cafeteria.' She bent over the bed and whispered: 'No, his wheelchair is still here.' She walked past Roger and Huyghe into the corridor. Without looking back, she let herself off the hook with: 'We can't keep every patient under constant surveillance, you know. But I do think it's strange we didn't see Mr. Maes leave.'

She took her place behind the counter and shrugged her shoulders.

'Come back in an hour. He's got an appointment with the doctor.'

Roger thanked her and hurried to the elevator.

'If Maes is in the cafeteria I'll eat my hat,' he growled while the elevator went, far too slowly, down to the ground floor.

◆

Wes got off the bus. The plastic bag cut into his fingers. He put it down and faced the turbines, like an Indian would a totem pole. The blades sliced through the heat. He had never seen them turn so fast, they had gone berserk. He closed his eyes and savored the sensation of the wind stroking his hair. The turbines did not hold him back. At most they would witness what was about to happen. Wes wiggled his fingers to get the circulation going again, and picked up the bag with his other hand.

The police cordon around the butcher shop flapped. But his destination was another house, across the road. Lucky break: the bus had crossed paths with the mailman. You always recognized that twerp by his dogged, clenched-teeth way of biking, as though he were about to win the sprint on the Champs-Elysées. The mop-head had sired two hot daughters, but aside from that Wes considered him a loser. Jeez, it was Saturday, and the guy was still on his bike. How freaky could you get. But Mister Speed Cyclist being out of the way made things definitely easier.

He set the bag down and took out the carton of eggs. The ripe tomatoes he'd save for later. His hands trembled, like the first time he opened a packet of cigarettes, when he tried to sneak his first smoke but his mother had stormed into his room after just three puffs. That's how long it took for the entire house to reek of his forbidden experiment. She was furious and gave him a clout. His mother, who now lay in a pool of vomit on the stairs.

He had never spoken to Magda De Gryse, whose house he was about to deface. She was one of those people he passed by on his way to more interesting ones. But now she did interest him. With his father in jail and his mother dead as a doornail, this woman deserved to be punished, in person, by Wes Bracke. She had ruined his life too. Now he didn't stand a chance with Machteld. If he ever were to have another relationship, it would be with a heroin whore, or a cheap, shabby tramp like the girl he'd rescued from the old geezer.

The egg felt pleasantly heavy in his hand. It was full to bursting. He aimed and threw. It spattered against a window with a dull thwack. A piece of shell trickled lazily down the pane. Nice. Wes took another egg. This one splattered just above the stain left by the first one. The third egg hit the front door, and the fourth landed smack in the mailbox. Awesome!

Wes changed tactics. He no longer wanted to save the tomatoes for later, he was too curious to see if they gave him as much satisfaction as the eggs. The first tomato hit the window with an enormous thud. He hoped the glass would shatter. When it did not, he threw a second tomato. Harder. It splattered against the wall. Bad aim. The third one hit the door. Kebang! The more he threw, the more pleasure it gave him. He wound up to lob the fourth tomato when the door opened.

'Will you cut that out!'

It was her. She came outside and had the nerve to reprimand him.

'What do you think you're doing!'

There she stood, the woman who'd ensured that he would never kiss Machteld, that he would never caress her breasts, that he would never feel the warmth of her thighs. She was wearing a flowered dress cut just above the knee. She had nice legs, and her cleavage suggested a full bosom. She was good-looking, for her age. Then she screamed at him a third time.

You learn to ride on an old bike. His father whispered it in his ear. The tomato whizzed through the air and hit Magda De Gryse squarely in the face. Screeching, she stumbled backward. Wes ran toward her.

Jan Lietaer couldn't believe his luck. The job notice hadn't hung there but half a day, and now he was already shaking hands with his new secretary. The girl's head bobbed up and down in synch. Her face glowed like that of a dog who'd just been tossed a barbecue sausage. Jan had no illusions about her abilities—he'd be happy if she even managed to get the coffee machine and the computer up and running—but she had agreed to the minimum wage (although he didn't refer to it as such) and was fond of animals. Who knows, maybe she was a quick learner. Perhaps she would charm the clients with her naive innocence. She might just surprise him.

'Then I'll see you Monday morning at eight-thirty for your first day at work,' Jan said as he led her outside. The sun's glare sliced open his headache.

'Thank you, Dr. Lietaer. I'm so looking forward to it. I won't disappoint you.' She blushed. She kept nodding. He smiled.

'I'm sure you won't,' he said. The girl went on her way. The smile vanished from Jan's lips when a sporty black Mercedes stopped at the door. His mother got out and her expression, as always, said she was on the warpath.

◆

Ivan crossed the street. He mustn't be there when the dog gobbled up the piece of farmer's sausage. The acetaminophen would do its work, not as quickly as with Magda De Gryse's cat, but within a few days the dog would be dead. The dose was high enough.

Ivan wanted to pay Mrs. Deknudt a visit. Old people: they liked to forget they owed you money. Once he'd taken care of that he could settle down for his afternoon nap. He had already rolled down the metal blinds to keep out the bright sunlight and the heat.

Further up, the police tape flapped in the breeze. *Haughtiness goeth before the fall.* Ivan's attention was fixed on Mrs. Deknudt's front door, which is why he did not see the stains on the De Gryse's window. Not that he cared, really. Ivan provided a service to his fellow townsfolk. Their personal lives did not interest him. Blaashoek's social life left him cold.

He rang the doorbell twice in quick succession. Otherwise Mrs. Deknudt might not answer the door. Since being swindled by a door-to-door salesman who talked her into buying 100 packs of toilet paper, Mrs. Deknudt only opened the door for people she knew, and who knew they had to ring twice. In practice these were the doctor and Ivan Camerlynck.

She did not answer the door. Perhaps she was on the toilet. Or dozing on the veranda, where she might not hear the bell. He rang again. Two short rings. He turned and looked back at the front of the pharmacy. Must get those upstairs windows painted. His gaze shifted to the building next door. The second-floor windows had modern curtains. No nude women to see on this side of the house then. Ivan grinned.

He rang again. Come on, Mrs. Deknudt, I don't have all day. Was she spying on him from behind the window? Did she refuse to answer the door because of her unsettled account? Then it was time for a more assertive approach.

He leaned forward and lifted the flap to the letter slot so he could call inside. Before he managed to get a word out of his throat, a fat housefly flew into his mouth. Five other flies escaped through the letter slot and vanished like felt-tip pen dots in the air. Ivan Camerlynck recoiled, retching.

◆

The dog lost its balance. He rolled over onto his side and urinated blood. Saliva frothed out of his open mouth. He tried to stand upright, but fell, wailing, onto his other side. The animal lay stock-still and made a strange rasping noise, as though he were choking. Catherine clapped her hands to her mouth.

'Bienvenue!'

The African came to her side. He followed her horrified gaze.

'*Mon Dieu*, what's wrong with that beast?'

'He's pissing blood! He's going to die!'

Bienvenue bounded across the room in three steps. She heard him rumble down the stairs. She followed him. On the ground floor there was a door to a courtyard they never used; it belonged to the girl's apartment. Bienvenue moved the garbage can and Catherine's bike out of the way and sprinted out back.

He tried to calm the animal. The gasping subsided.

'Will he make it?' Catherine's voice cracked.

'*Sais pas.*' Bienvenue stroked the fur. He scanned the battleground where the little dog was fighting for his life. Then he picked something up off the ground. A short stump. He sniffed it and raised his eyebrows.

'What is it?' Catherine asked.

'*Saucisse.*'

'Poisoned?'

'I don't smell anything strange.'

The butcher was in jail, so it couldn't have been him. Claire? Even though rumor had it she had murdered Magda's cat, right now she had other things on her mind than killing that girl's dog. Ivan Camerlynck, Catherine thought. That filthy bastard.

◆

Ivan teetered. He had swallowed a fly that just been savoring Mrs. Deknudt's dead body. A thin stream of sourness spattered onto the sidewalk. He recognized ground meat and mashed potatoes. It tasted of half-digested applesauce.

Tears of disgust prickled his eyes. He panted, bent over with his hands on his knees. Must call the police. He was just about to cross the street when a blonde woman emerged from number 27 and approached him. Wasn't that the Lietaer woman? She looked as slovenly as that hussy from the ground floor.

'Call the police!' he shouted. 'Mrs. Deknudt is dead!'

'You dirty, stinking son of a bitch!' the woman yelled back.

◆

Saskia Maes beamed. Imagine it having gone so smoothly! At last she had begun her climb up the social ladder. Her life—she'd taken it into her own hands. Now she was part of the real world. She would earn money. She would save, she would pay her own rent, she might buy a house one day. She wanted to be the best secretary Dr. Lietaer ever dreamed of. Spending every day among all those house pets, what a marvelous prospect! She giggled. She no longer walked, she skipped. Above the rooftops the turbines waved, and Saskia waved back. She danced, no, she floated into the grocer's. She deserved an indulgence, and above all she wanted to surprise Zeppos with a treat. Because thanks to her darling pet, she had ended up at the vet's. Zeppos was going to have the best day of his life.

◆

'What's this?' His mother snatched the sheet of paper out of his hand. Jan had just peeled it off the window. Now she looked up at him inquiringly.

'Why are you looking for a secretary?'

He turned away before her eyes burned holes in his face.

'I'm not looking for a secretary. I've already found one.'

'Can't Catherine do it anymore?'

He went over to the window.

'Catherine has left me.'

In the ensuing silence he could feel her contempt intensify. She had the humiliating talent of turning silences into insults.

'She's leaving you?'

He had to repeat it. She sniffed. She probably no longer noticed the fog of perfume that hung around her like a cloud of poisonous gas.

'I knew she would. She was too posh for you. What you need is a frump, not a model.'

Jan did not answer. Posh—if she only knew. He let her rant. His mother was only out to rile him, and the sooner she got what she wanted, the sooner she'd leave.

'You have no ambition, Jan. You're dull, you're a bore. A woman needs excitement, you have to stimulate her, you have to surprise her, every day. You dilly-dally around with a half-baked veterinary practice, you spend hours on end weeding that backyard of yours, or shoot holes in tin cans like a child. There's not a woman on earth who'd put up with it!'

Despite his growing ire, he held his tongue. He could tell, from her breathing and shuffling, that it irritated her. She was a wild cat, waiting impatiently until her prey got close enough to pounce on it.

'Do you know who it is? Do you know who your wife's run off with?'

'No, I don't. But I've taken all the necessary measures. The lawyer's been informed, and I have a new secretary.'

His mother smirked and let the paper with the job notice flutter to the floor. It came to rest alongside his feet. She went over next to him; her poison nebule made his head spin.

'Typical, Jan. *So* typical. You just give in. You don't put up a fight. You're spineless. She's going to fleece you, because that's what happens to losers. And you are a born loser!'

She stood there glowering at him.

'Well, are you going to do something?' she demanded. 'Or are you going to stand here gawking at your backyard? And at your windmill?'

Her heels tortured the floor tiles, her laugh tortured his humor. The door slammed shut. She emphasized her departure by flooring it as she drove off. Jan cursed and pounded his fist against the window. Every second, a shadow swept across the lawn. He was fed up. Whatever he did, it was always wrong.

He was fed up!

Fed! Up!

He opened the gun cabinet, took out the Remington Rand M1911A1 and ran out into the yard. He pointed the pistol at the turbine and with the words 'fucking turbine!' he fired four shots.

◆

'What did you do to that dog, you bastard?'

Catherine stormed over to the pharmacist and gave him a shove. That sweaty body of his disgusted her. Camerlynck stumbled backward. He tried to catch himself, but grasped at thin air and landed clumsily on his backside. He was wearing gray woolen winter socks and worn-out shoes. In this weather. Camerlynck scrabbled upright.

'Keep your hands off me, bitch. I don't know anything about a dog.'

'You know full well what I'm talking about, poison-mixer,' Catherine snapped. 'The dog that belongs to the girl downstairs from Bienvenue. He was choking on a piece of sausage just now.'

'Nothing to do with me.' He nervously tucked his shirt back into his trousers. The collar was gray instead of white.

'Coward.'

'Ah, shut your trap, slut,' Camerlynck hissed. 'Go suck your afro-cock.'

'What did you say?'

Catherine stepped toward him. But he was quicker, and

pushed her into the street. She lost her balance and fell onto the asphalt. The same fear gripped her as when she was pushed into a swimming pool. Now she did not fear drowning, but rather being run over by the car that came squealing to a halt. The bumper came to a standstill not ten centimeters from her face. She could count the mud flecks on the license plate. She sat up and looked at the grille. It was a Mercedes. A grumpy old man opened the driver's door and hobbled over to her.

'Now, little lady, this is no place to be sunbathing.'

He helped her up. She nodded politely, checked for any other approaching cars and hurried back to Bienvenue's.

◆

Ivan guessed dark green, but the Mercedes was so caked with mud that the original color could just as well be gray or dark blue. An old farmer helped the Lietaer woman to her feet, after which she dashed across the road and disappeared into the house. Not such a big mouth all of a sudden, the craven slut.

'Afternoon,' the farmer said. Ivan nodded.

'Sir,' the farmer continued, 'might you know which of these is the subsidized housing?'

Ivan pointed to the house where the Lietaer bitch had fled. That he had once fantasized about her, he now found unthinkable.

'There,' he said. 'Where the woman you nearly ran over went.'

'If you don't want to get run over, you shouldn't lie in the middle of the road,' the farmer grumbled.

'Right you are, sir. Ah, it's always that type who disrupt things. Your car could have been damaged, or she'd have come after you with a lawsuit.'

The farmer laughed.

'Lawsuits—I wipe me ass with them. I settle my own business, like in the old days.'

He walked around to the back of his rust bucket and opened the trunk.

'The house next door to the pharmacy, you say?'

'That's right,' said Ivan.

'You go on home, mister,' the farmer said to Ivan as he rummaged around in the trunk. 'This is going to be no sight for sensitive eyes.' An unctuous laugh hung in the air as Ivan hurried off.

◆

The first two bullets whizzed past the turbine, one landing in Farmer Pouseele's field and the other in the crown of an old beech tree. The next two hit the turbine with a sharp metallic tick. They ricocheted off it. The first one went off in a northerly direction and ended up in a clod of earth along the Blaashoek Canal. The last bullet swerved off toward the town and killed a person.

Jan Lietaer took a deep breath and sighed. What in heaven's name was he doing, shooting at that stupid turbine? He knew of a far better target! He looked from the gun to the turbine. With a light heart he ran out onto the street.

◆

There were three varieties of canned food: turkey with carrots, veal in sauce, and beef with noodles. The small tubs in the next rack appealed to Saskia more: Mediterranean lamb, beef with Italian pasta, and chicken-vegetable pâté. Zeppos deserved the most delicious meal of his life and they hadn't made her choice any easier.

The cans contained more food and were four times as cheap, but the tubs looked so delicious. A cute little dog smiled out at her from the label. He looked so happy, with his sparkling eyes and that pink tongue hanging out of his mouth. She wanted to see Zeppos just as elated. She counted the coins in her purse twice, took a tub of the beef with Italian pasta, tried not to look at the price and went to the bakery department. She ordered an éclair; the sensation of being an indulgent greedy-guts made her blush. Dorien Chielens told her she was supposed to enjoy life, that she could treat herself to a little extravagance once in a while, that it wasn't wrong to let loose sometimes. Particularly on a special day—and this was indeed a special day. Wouldn't Dorien be impressed if she heard Saskia had found a job!

Smiling from ear to ear, Saskia stepped outside. The smile was still on her face when Jan Lietaer's ricocheted bullet fatally struck her, at the happiest moment of her life. She collapsed face-first onto the sidewalk and a tub of dog food rolled out of her hand.

Through her tears she could only see a dark patch where Bienvenue stood. The patch grew until it filled her entire field of vision. She felt the muscles in his arms.

'He ...'

'I'll take care of this,' Bienvenue said.

She did not have the energy to restrain him.

Roger turned onto the Blaashoekstraat and recognized the brawny figure hobbling across the street, a double-barreled shotgun cradled tightly against his body.

'God damn it,' Roger cursed. He turned on the siren, but this had no effect whatsoever on Farmer Maes.

'Put down that weapon!' Huyghe's voice echoed the length of the Blaashoekstraat. Then the front door opened.

A black man came out. It was too late for warnings. Roger braked, grabbed his gun and jumped out of the patrol car.

◆

Jan Lietaer cursed. There was only one bullet left in the Remington Rand, and he just realized he had *two* choice targets. Well, the decision would be a quick one: whichever of those lovebirds first crossed his path was a goner.

His lousy condition forced him to slacken his pace from a jog to a firm tread. He resolved to spend some time on the home trainer before hunting season began. It could just be this hellish heat. And that incessant wind.

There was a commotion outside the grocer's. Patricia, the shopkeeper, stood in the doorway gesticulating wildly with one arm while shouting into a cordless telephone. A girl lay at her feet. She seemed to have fainted, but the blood that leaked out from under her body into the gutter made one fear the worst. The very worst. Jan ran over to the girl.

The woman from the grocery was screaming hysterically.

'She fell! She left the store and fell! Oh God, all that blood!'

Now he recognized Saskia Maes. He felt her neck, his hand got covered in blood. A weak pulse. Her eyes were bulging and glassy. Jesus, what on earth happened here?

She whispered. Zep, Zep, Zep.

'Shh, Saskia, everything will be all right.'

Her eyes rolled back in their sockets, he saw only the whites. She was losing too much blood. It soaked into his shirt, into his trousers. It also soaked into his soul, for just as Saskia's blood flowed out of her body, the anger flowed out of his own, his fury against Catherine and her Negro, a fury that now seemed to have come from another world.

'Put down that weapon!'

Jan looked up, startled. For a moment he thought the voice from the patrol car was addressing him. Then he saw an old man cross the street. He was carrying a double-barreled rifle, a Blaser, Jan guessed. Had the old guy shot Saskia? He must have. A policeman jumped out from the driver's side.

Across the street, a black man emerged from number 27.

'Bienvenue!' Jan shouted.

The black man looked at him, just for a few seconds, and then his head turned into an explosion of flesh, bones and blood.

◆

Compare it to a churlish dog. It couldn't be trusted, no matter how much energy you put into it. An unreliable animal is a useless animal. You have to kill it. Maybe the sissified city folk thought an animal was meant to be cuddled, but he at least still knew what animals were for: the cat catches mice, the dog guards the farm, the pig provides pork chops. And the woman keeps house. Saskia had become unreliable, just like her mother. There was no saving her. He could just as well put an end to it, while the family honor was still more or less intact.

He was annoyed by the hip that tugged sorely at his nerves. He did not want to call it pain. Pain was for women and queers.

The door to the house opened. Good, now he didn't have to ring the bell. A large Negro man came toward him. He shot.

◆

Bienvenue needed time to orient himself. To his left there was a police car, from which two officers sprang. And from the right he heard someone call his name. Was that Catherine's husband? And was he really pointing a gun? Good God, the man wasn't going to make a scene, was he?

Bienvenue's head exploded before he could realize the danger did not come from Jan Lietaer. His body took two more steps before it collapsed.

◆

Jan gagged. What kind of nightmare had he landed in?

'Put down that weapon!' The policewoman's voice trembled when the farmer turned and pointed his rifle at them. Just in time, Jan remembered his Remington Rand. He took it and shot. He missed the farmer. One of the windows of the patrol car shattered and the policeman was buried, cursing, under the shards of glass.

◆

Farmer Maes didn't have much time. The male cop wanted to blow him away, but somehow managed to shoot his own window to smithereens. That's modern police for you, bunch of meter maids. He did not worry about the other officer, it was a woman. He aimed at the open front door again, stepped over the body of the black man and quickened his pace.

◆

Roger Hauspie cut his fingers on the glass as he swept it out of his hair. There was blood on his forehead. Worry about that later. He dived back into the patrol car and reached for the radio. He requested reinforcement and saw that Huyghe was gone.

◆

He followed his instinct. The downstairs apartment appeared empty. He bounded up the stairs. He smelled her fear, he sensed her apprehension. A trapped animal. Nothing finer than an animal that knows it's about to die.

'Did you really think you could escape?' Farmer Maes shouted. 'Did you really think you could just walk away, you stupid goat?' He held the double-barreled shotgun firmly in his big hands. He was far enough up the stairs to see into the landing. The door to the apartment was open. He heard stumbling and whimpering. His instinct had not failed him. His instinct never failed him.

'You asked for it, Saskia! It's your own fault!'

◆

Catherine saw it happen from behind the curtain in Bienvenue's apartment. She saw the stinking farmer wave his double-barreled rifle, she saw the police car brake. Suddenly Bienvenue was standing under the window. She screamed when the farmer shot, and screamed even louder when she saw what happened to Bienvenue. When the policeman ducked out of the patrol car, she herself ducked behind the sofa and crawled on her hands and knees to the bedroom. She heard another shot and hoped the policeman had taken out that crazy farmer. Just to be sure, she remained crouched behind the bed, her eyes glued to the open door that led to the hallway. She trembled. She prayed that the first person she saw would be wearing a police uniform.

◆

Roger Hauspie leaned back. The fact that reinforcements were on their way did not reassure him. It could take them ten minutes to get here, and in those ten minutes he was unable to come to Huyghe's aid. Blood trickled under the hand he held against his forehead, it stung his eyes, making it impossible for Roger to recognize the man who appeared in the passenger seat of the patrol car.

'I do apologize, officer,' the man panted. His voice trembled. 'I wanted to shoot that lunatic, and hit your car by mistake.'

'That's what you get for trying to play the hero,' Roger snarled. He tasted something metallic, as though he were sucking on a spoon.

'I really am terribly sorry. Let me have a look at your injuries.'

Roger felt the man's hands probe his head.

'It looks worse than it is,' the man mumbled. Roger heard the man unbutton his shirt and tear off a piece, which he pressed against the wound.

'Hold this tight.'

Hauspie grunted.

The man made a move to leave the car. 'I'm going to —'

'Oh no! You're not going to do anything! You've caused enough damage already. You're waiting here with me until the reinforcements arrive. If you leave this vehicle, I'll shoot you. I might not be able to aim, but I'll make damn sure I hit you.'

The man slid back into the passenger seat. He sighed, which irked Hauspie even more.

'And if anything happens to Huyghe, you're dead meat.'

◆

Catherine clutched the bedsheets and pressed her nose into the mattress, which became wet with her tears. Her soul clung to the scent of the sheets, her own scent and that of the man lying down there on the sidewalk, and an odd serenity befell her. Was this the punishment for her adultery? Was there such a thing as a divine power who passed judgment on good and evil, and who had sent this farmer to her from hell? She heard him shout a string of abuse before the landing creaked under his weight. Then he appeared in the hall. She screamed as he pointed his weapon at her.

◆

It wasn't Saskia. It was that broad who'd thrown herself in front of his car. She crouched there yowling, the mad-woman. He cursed.

'Saskia, where are you?'

He turned back toward the front door of the apartment. Was she downstairs after all? Had that serpent given him the slip? He heard the stairs creak. Was she trying to escape? He ran out onto the landing.

'Where are you, you dirty slut!'

He got no further than that.

◆

Three shots rang out. Catherine dug her nails into the sheets. Through her tears she saw the ungainly figure of the old man collapse into the hall. A muffled thud and he disappeared from view. Was he dead? She heard nothing save the thumping of her own heart. Snot and tears—there was no holding them back now—soaked the sheets. She breathed heavily through her mouth, and her crying was soundless.

A second figure came into the hall. It hesitated briefly, and then approached. Catherine recognized a police uni-form.

'I'm sorry,' Catherine blubbered. 'I'm so sorry.'

'Shh now,' the woman said, taking her in her arms. 'It's over.'

◆

Wes realized it was futile. He had already tried to enter Magda De Gryse a few times, but now his dick was limp, and limp it would stay. He swore. He had beaten her senseless and dragged her to the sofa, where he peeled her dress up over her head. A dark-red stain had seeped into the fabric, a combination of blood and tomato juice.

His erection was painfully hard while he pulled off her panties. Unable to get the clasp undone, he had slid the bra clumsily up over her breasts. Once she finally lay there, groaning and nearly naked, he didn't know what to do. Her body was less attractive than he had expected (a large scar marred her stomach), but the prospect of sex nevertheless wound him up. He felt her breasts and grabbled in her pubic hair. He rubbed her labia, which were soft and dry. Then he took off his pants and lay on top of her, but his dick wouldn't go in. This was supposed to be easy: in the porn videos his schoolmates sent him, the cocks plunged in as though the pussies simply sucked them up. His dick had gone soft and he had to tug at it for a full five minutes to get it back up again. The second attempt failed, as did the third. It was futile.

He cursed her. This bitch had ruined everything for him. He pulled his pants up. His father in jail, his mother dead, Machteld a lost cause, and now she foiled his well-deserved attempt at losing his virginity. He picked up a candlestick from the window sill, and it crossed his mind to give her body a good going-over with it.

A siren wailed, surprisingly close by.

Startled, he looked behind him, into the backyard. Had the police surrounded the house?

Then there was a shot.

'Put down that weapon!'

Another shot.

He ducked, crept to the hallway, and cautiously opened

the front door. A patrol car was parked further up. Through the rear window he couldn't tell if there was anyone inside. As he walked in the opposite direction, another three shots rang out. In the distance he heard more sirens. He broke into a run. At the Blaashoek Canal he paused. The blades of the turbines turned languidly, as in slow motion. The movement comforted him, as though the turbines slowed down time, giving him the chance to escape. When he left Blaashoek, he did not look back.

◆

His head in a cloud of contemplation, Walter De Gryse cycled along the Blaashoek Canal. Come Monday he might have lost his job, because a Limburger with more fantasy than compassion felt it necessary to file a complaint with the police. Public indecency, come on … Walter shook his head. He looked down the embankment, toward the dock. The Egoist was gone. Typical. Get other people into trouble and then sneak off. What made people do this kind of thing? Bully each other in a bout of rashness, kill each other off in a fit of rage. He stopped. Was there anything left to see of his mishap? No. Nature, he mused, is a wondrous thing.

Were those gunshots he heard? He pricked up his ears. They came from the direction of Jan Lietaer's house. Maybe he was practicing for hunting season. Then it went quiet again, except for the rippling of the water, the occasional animal sound, the rustling of the wind.

Now a siren, just for a few seconds, and another shot. He looked back, but the road to Blaashoek was empty. The town lay serenely under the leaden sun. He must have imagined it. He hadn't slept much last night. The whole town probably slept badly, after that terrible news about Herman. Herman, his good-natured neighbor. Who'd have thought?

Magda, maybe.

She had noticed there was something up with Herman. Magda was a hard woman, at times she harbored a stubborn and unreasonable prejudice against someone. But she was usually right. How often had Walter secretly scoffed at her hunch that Herman and Claire were responsible for the murder of Minous? Now it was starting to sound perfectly plausible. If Herman was capable of chopping a food inspector into pieces without batting an eye, what's to stop him from poisoning the neighbor's cat? Walter shuddered, while in his fantasy he heard three more gunshots.

Just as he put his foot back on the pedal, a wail of sirens wafted over from the city. The squall came closer.

'People are monsters,' Walter said under his breath.

He looked at the turbines. The blades stood still.

He closed his eyes. He opened them again.

The turbines were motionless. Like they were frozen.

He put his foot on the pedal. Water lapped against the dock, the buttercups on the bank swayed. The wind tussled his curls, but the turbines remained still.

Maybe he should also take a time out in his own life. Maybe it was finally the moment for them to travel to the pearly-white beaches he'd dreamed of as a child. After everything that had happened, a change of scenery would do them good.

He was getting hungry. He felt like a sandwich. Without summer pâté, from now on.

Under the crescendo of the sirens, he cycled homeward.

On the Design

As book design is an integral part of the reading experience, we would like to acknowledge the work of those who shaped the form in which the story is housed.

Tessa van der Waals (Netherlands) is responsible for the cover design, cover typography and art direction of all World Editions books. She works in the internationally renowned tradition of Dutch Design. Her bright and powerful visual aesthetic maintains a harmony between image and typography and captures the unique atmosphere of each book. She works closely with internationally celebrated photographers, artists, and letter designers. Her work has frequently been awarded prizes for Best Dutch Book Design.

Mischa Keijser is a Dutch artist and photographer who regularly exhibits and publishes his work. His relationship to Dutch nature and landscape is a major theme, and he often includes elements of his personal life in his images. It took several attempts to get the perfect shot for the cover image; Mischa had to travel from the Netherlands to Belgium with his daughter more than once because the weather was too beautiful, before finally returning on the evening of an approaching storm. 'My daughter had to run back and forth—on each occasion—at least 50 times. In addition to bouts of jumping, standing stock still, and trying out various methods of falling over on purpose.'

The cover has been edited by lithographer Bert van der Horst of BFC Graphics (Netherlands).

Suzan Beijer (Netherlands) is responsible for the typography and careful interior book design of all World Editions titles.

The text on the inside covers and the press quotes are set in Circular, designed by Laurenz Brunner (Switzerland) and published by Swiss type foundry Lineto.

All World Editions books are set in the typeface Dolly, specifically designed for book typography. Dolly creates a warm page image perfect for an enjoyable reading experience. This typeface is designed by Underware, a European collective formed by Bas Jacobs (Netherlands), Akiem Helmling (Germany), and Sami Kortemäki (Finland). Underware are also the creators of the World Editions logo, which meets the design requirement that 'a strong shape can always be drawn with a toe in the sand.'